POETRY
LOVER

Books by Gary Soto

Gary Soto

UNIVERSITY OF NEW MEXICO PRESS

ALBUQUERQUE

Library of Congress Cataloging-in-Publication Data

Soto, Gary
     Poetry Lover / Gary Soto. — 1st ed.
         p. cm.
     ISBN 0-8263-2319-7 (alk. paper)
  1. Mexican American poets—Fiction. I. Title
   PS3569.072 P64 2001
   813′ .54—dc21

                                      00-010700

A portion of this novel appeared in *The Santa Monica Review*, spring 2000,
and is reprinted here with their permission.

This is a work of fiction. Any resemblance to any person,
living or dead, is coincidental.

Design: Mina Yamashita

To Scott Brown,
book collector extraordinaire
&
Martín Espada,
poet extraordinaire

S ilver Mendez scowled as he considered the photo on his expired passport. His face was small and—God, yes—his eyes revealed a hint of defeat, tiny portholes unlit and dark as ash. True, his face was unlined, babyish, even. His cheeks were not yet dragged down by the gravity of his near homeless-ness, a growing concern because on more than one occasion he had been forced to carry a sleeping bag through a park full of hoodlums and pitch himself under the wheeling stars. He was twenty something in the photo and was quickly headed nowhere in spite of his stature as a Chicano poet with two poetry books. True, one book was a staple job assembled like tacos in the kitchen of a friend of a friend, but its forty-eight pages were evidence of more toil than some Chicano Studies profs with nothing to show but the bulky waistlines of middle income. Once, when he was put on the spot about his accomplishments in this newly founded literature, he hammered his fist against his chest and bragged, "I'm the first Chicano to write in complete sentences."

That was seventeen years ago, when patches of sunshine splashed the trees and spread their crowning warmth on his shiny head. When there had been a jump in his step and a roar in his voice. Change had clapped in his pockets. The arms of young women had snaked around his waist and brought him to his grateful knees so they could lap his neck with their pink tongues. He was known in some literary and artistic circles and was a near winner of a literary prize—or so rumor had it. He had aired his opinions many times on KPFA and was cool enough not to hog the microphone at numerous open mike performances in dirty restaurants. But now, at thirty-nine, with a hairline receding like the sea at low tide and with his belt noosed on its last hole, he had only to consider where, when, or why he woke.

But today a marvelous piece of luck. A thin letter, noisy as cellophane, arrived at his mother's house in West Oakland, a miracle in itself because from what he surmised in his jaunts from home to the bus stop, most postal carriers slept in their Jeeps until quitting time. In ornate academic Spanish, the letter invited him to Madrid in April to participate in a conference on Chicano literature. When he first read the letter, Silver was forced to employ his dictionary to decipher the stilted language and had problems with the use of the subjunctive. But he understood from the get-go that someone in Spain requested his presence, a wholly new experience. On the streets of San Francisco and Oakland his friends, rags themselves blowing in the wind, hobbled away when they saw him coming. The letter requested his e-mail address, a big laugh for Silver because not only did he lack a computer, or an outlet to plug it into, but also a typewriter, electric or manual. His only ways of reaching the outside world were a nibbled pencil and a nearly bloodless Bic pen he had to shake like a madman. The cold weather had clogged its vein of ink.

The letter writer was a woman named Olga Alvarez Moreno, assistant professor of modern languages at the University of Salamanca. With his palms itching, Silver marveled at his luck. When had he last received a letter from a professor of Hispanic literature? He closed his eyes, assembling her character—early thirties, honey tanned, unmarried but hurt by a caustic lover, and with long, brownish hair on which sunglasses sat smartly. He imagined her pulling the sunglasses off her lovely head and clacking the earpieces between her upper and lower teeth. He shivered when he pictured her biting down on the earpiece.

He returned all too quickly from his dream. With a finger, he petted the picture on his expired passport and swallowed a garlic clove of sorrow. His youth had passed. In his mind's eye, he was still twenty years old, but the heart knew better: Those sunny days were over, replaced—literally, as rain drummed on his mother's roof—by clouds that boiled and darkened on a never-ending afternoon. But the letter from Salamanca lifted Silver's sagging spirit. All he needed was a new passport and a thousand dollars to carry him off to Madrid, city of bloated wineskins, tapas, and castanets chattering like dentures. He smiled. He sang, "The rain in Spain falls mainly on the plain ole me. He he he."

When his mother entered the living room, pins in her mouth and his torn shirt in her hands, he shoved the expired passport into his back pocket. His mother suspiciously narrowed her work-ravaged eyes at him.

"What are you doing?" she asked sourly. She stood over the floor furnace, her orange bathrobe billowing about her legs. Broom or no broom, she looked ready to lift off the carpeted floor, toes wiggling, and begin flying about the living room.

"Nothing."

Immediately Silver gauged his error.

"That's about right—nada!" His mother mumbled other blasting truths without taking the pins from her mouth. To Silver, his mother seemed like a voodoo doll—scary. He couldn't understand being born of such flesh, for she could barely put two nice words together, while he had spent his whole life—the last twenty years, anyway—making poetry . . . for the people.

Silver would have parried her evaluation of his life thus far, but he was in such a good mood that he let her taunts pass. He sat on the couch, hands folded on the valley of his sunken stomach, and ignored his mother as she angrily mended his shirt, ripped when he hurled himself over a chain-link fence. The cause of the rip was a former friend to whom he owed money, the same person who, in 1975, footed the printing of his first book of poems, *Tigres en Armas*, by strong-arming friends and collecting *el dinero* in a half-gallon milk carton. This person, Al Sanchez, now a body-and-fender man but once a drummer in a Chicano rock group called Cambio Rama, hankered to beat his ass for failing to cough up a three-year-old debt of two hundred dollars. Silver sensed that Al was just starved to body punch whatever unfortunate acquaintance sauntered his way. When he happened to stroke into the Dip and Wash Laundromat on a bland Sunday, Silver was an easy and justifiable target.

"Hey," Silver greeted Al. Silver had forgotten the debt. By nature, he forgot all debts after one week.

"'Hey,' my ass!" Al raged, clutching his wife's bra, huge holsters that held a mass of brown skin (Silver had slept with her and knew from firsthand experience the taste of those tart buns). Al slapped the bra against the folding table and took after Silver, who, bug-eyed, dropped his bundle of sour clothes, mostly whites the color of bad teeth. He failed to scissor more than a half-dozen steps before Al gripped him by his bony shoulder. Known as a strong drummer, particularly during his hour-long solos, during which time his band members would leave the stage to smoke joints, he proved the rumors true as he beat Silver like a tom-tom.

Silver didn't have the chance to wail, "That hurts," or, "Let's be friends and get a soda, on me." He didn't cry a word because most of the air inside him had been expelled by a swift punch to his ribs. The palm strike to his diaphragm didn't help either. More air gushed from the dark cavern right below his heart. If he had been a blown-up doll, Silver would have collapsed spinelessly onto the dirty floor.

But by accident—or so he would tell Al if he later encountered him on the streets—Silver elbowed his beastly opponent in his left eye, a blow with surprising strength and purpose at the receiving end. Al let out a preliminary "ouch," followed by, "You shithead." He bowed his head and squinted until his vision returned, albeit watery.

"I'm sorry," Silver apologized. He picked up one of the bras and tried to hand it back to his creditor, but Al, a hunchback in pain, wouldn't have it.

Al growled.

Silver again begged forgiveness, turned with the bra still in his hand, and ran down Foothill Avenue, without question the fastest poet of all time. He made his way into a parking lot of the bar El Gordito, where three brown drunks staggered like bowling pins ready to topple. He ripped his shirt while climbing a chain-link fence. But he would run until he was naked because he knew better than to anger Al. The guy knew genuine thugs and glue-demented *vatos locos*.

But now, with this letter from Spain, his boat had tooted and finally docked. Hope seemed real, not a dreamy mirage. As he sat in the living room with his mother, he promised himself to get his act together. True, he had never known his father and never inquired about his where-abouts. To do so would either bring on rage or a teary con-fession from his mother about his father's inability to nurture a family life for his son. He wanted neither that evening. He wanted money.

"Mom," Silver called softly.

His mother's eyes floated up from her sewing.

"Lend me a thousand dollars."

Her eyes floated down. Her hands tightened on the shirt collar she was mending; if Silver's neck had been stuffed in it, he would be blue in the face and near death. Certainly blood would have spurted when she brought the shirt to her mouth and bit off the thread. She put the pins back in her lined mouth.

He swallowed and tried again. He brought out the let-ter from Spain, rattled it at her, and told her that Profesora Olga Alvarez Moreno, a real intelligent gal from the look of things, had invited him to a conference on Chicano literature. What better way to start anew than to go abroad, freshen his worldly vision while eating plate after plate of tapas, and mingle with smart people?

"Smart people!" She spit the pins out of her mouth, daggers that fell within inches of Silver's feet. "You're almost forty! You're lazy, not smart! You don't have a pot to pee in but your hands!"

Silver's hair nearly stood up from her blasting candor. His ears rang like crickets. Sourness began to pipe in his stomach. He had to get up and go into the kitchen, where he fixed himself a cocktail of water, ice, and a slice of lemon. He sipped his drink while he studied the patio, presently a two-inch lake of dark rain. He meditated on Noah's ark, more precisely on how the animals were paired off—two elephants, two squirrels, two armadillos, two of everything. If by chance he ever boarded a modern version of Noah's ark, he would go alone.

Silver remembered leaving a box of *Tigres en Armas* in the rafters of the garage. He pushed his feet into his shoes, curled boats, and stepped out onto the back porch. The shoes carried him over the water that had gathered in the patio and was threatening to run into the garage. A rubber thong floated in a puddle. A bleach bottle bobbed like a buoy.

"That's enough," he scolded the sky. Then he reconsidered: No, the sky doesn't have ears, and if God does, then they must be plugged with wax. Otherwise wouldn't He respond to our grief? Wouldn't He be nice for once and make the rain become coins? The drought would be over for his kind—the poor with no other ambition but to park themselves in a hammock and swing in the wind.

He was about to curse at the rain, but he suddenly became mindful of its blessings for both man and animal, and the numerous plants, his favorite being the kingly pomegranate, though the watermelon—the Humpty-Dumpty of low-lying fruits—wasn't bad either. He felt he had to get out of the house and do something, anything, a feeling that had intensified when his mother had come into the kitchen still sporting pins in her mouth, though the shirt had been mended. She took the pins and stabbed them into the piggy pin cushion, an action brutal enough to make piggy cough up sawdust.

In the garage, he leaned a wooden ladder against the rafters and climbed carefully, his head basking in the warm air that circulated at that height. He scanned the warm environs where sat cans of paint and paint thinner, and he saw in the shadows the single remaining toy from his childhood—a hobbyhorse with the mane of a dirty restaurant mop.

He struggled with the box and sneezed twice because what he was touching was ancient and dusty—his first poetry book. His intention was to peddle his lost book if he was able to get a college poetry reading. But when he opened the box, it was like gazing at his own bones after his body had shed its flesh. He picked up a mildewed book with staples brown with rust. He read the first stanza of one poem but snapped the book closed when he came to the lines: "O race of coffee skin/hence forward *la raza* you shall be called. Busted are the chains! Busted!"

"Was I that awful?" he asked himself, suddenly frightened by what had come from his youthful pen and was presently embedded in the memories of people who occasionally remembered him in—good God—fits of laughter? He would have searched those metaphors for meaning, but he was overwhelmed by the desire to separate the past from where he now stood, on the third rung of a wobbly, wooden ladder. He flicked the book into the box and shoved it back into the rafters. If he could be sure that they would disappear altogether, he would have set the whole bunch of poems on an ark and let them float away from their busted chains. But he couldn't take that chance. He set the box next to his hobbyhorse and clip-clopped back through the rain to the house. He escaped to bed and hoped not to recall in his dreams that brief encounter with his first effort at poetry—in print, too! He fell

asleep grimacing at the sound of bedsheets and towels being ripped into bandages for dogs and cats at the Humane
Society. This was his mother's once-a-month gift to the furry
world—cloth for bleeding and defecating animals. His sleep
was fitful as she worked until two in the morning.

Money was on Silver's mind when he left his mother's
house the next morning, a heaping bowl of shredded wheat
piled in his stomach and scouring, he visualized, the insides of his guts. He had to forage around for a thousand
dollars, possibly more. The plane ticket would run about
six hundred and, once there, in the land of "rain on the
plain," he needed a place to stay—he couldn't share a park
bench with Spain's homeless. What would the intellectu-
als think? He, a poet of Aztlán, with his pockets turned
inside out and nothing to show but a tooth-nibbled pencil. Moreover, he wouldn't dare boot some scarecrow of a
compañero from a park bench. For Christ's sake, he was a
sort of ambassador, not a freeloader.

I'll get a job, he told himself as he leapt over a puddle
on his way to Foothill Avenue. He would recap tires in
the factories of hell, drive a bulldozer into the side of a
mountain, and even shovel a swimming pool with a tin
cup. He was meaning to work and make up for lost time.

But by the time he leapt a third, Texas-shaped puddle, he dismissed real work in which his body would become shiny with sweat as unfair to his creative soul. The Madrid conference was in late April, less than three months away, and he didn't have time to find a job, one that required a windup alarm clock to rattle his bones awake. No, he must shake the easiest money tree of all—he had to get some college poetry readings. His last reading had been at a community college for three hundred dollars. And lucky him, he also got a date, but that one-night affair didn't go far, just heavy petting in a borrowed station wagon. There would have been more than undone snaps, buttons, and zippers had it not been for a squeaky Ford Pinto that pulled up next to them with the riffraff inside snickering. The moon was ogling, too, old man moon the biggest voyeur of both present and ancient times. Its brightness beamed into the car like a searchlight, shining on the beautiful left breast he had taken into his mouth—his head was a radish compared to that tremendous gift of nature that exuded a buttery taste. The date ended at Casper's on Telegraph Avenue, where Silver splurged on two hot dogs layered with the works.

The rain had stopped sometime before sunrise, moving east into the valley, where it hosed off the little cow towns and offered a respite from the aroma of hay, sump tanks, and pig slaughter. Drops of rain clung like jewels on even the scrawniest bushes, and sparrows, hoodlums on sycamore trees, trumpeted from the high branches. Somewhere a church bell rang for nine o'clock mass. Somewhere laughter echoed in a school yard, where the tykes were rechalking the grounds for a game of hopscotch. In spite of his mother's two-fisted attack the night before, Silver was so happy that he tapped the shirt pocket where he kept the letter from Spain. He began to jog. He leapt over one puddle and the next, although he did have to scoot around one oily lagoon that resembled Lake Michigan and on which floated an armada of soggy leaves. It was while jumping over another puddle that he became aware of someone keeping pace next to him. He turned to the fellow, who was blue-eyed and barrel-chested. He sported a head like a canned ham and was thick in arm and leg. And while Silver was breathing like a locomotive in the cool February air, the meathead's breathing was nearly invisible, like cigarette smoke long ago broken apart. The man was in good shape, Silver noted in awe, if only because of the massive block of his shoulders. It would be a workout in itself to balance that mass throughout the day.

Silver had plans to slow to a walk after the last puddle, but with the meathead running next to him, he hitched up his pants and sped up in spite of the huge army jacket that weighed like lead on his muscle-depleted ribs. The mysterious fellow, in turn, sped up with ease and soon both were jumping puddles like gazelles. Silver was becoming winded, though not so much that he dared slow down. He was even trying to speed up when the man asked, "Is your name Silvester Mendez?"

"Who you?" Silver asked. Too winded to form a complete sentence, he dropped the verb of being, something he often did in poetry because, he argued philosophically, that was how he and others spoke. It was then that he observed on the other side another man, also with a head like a canned ham, running up to him: The three appeared to be jogging in formation. This new person, however, was a Latino with a thin mustache. His face was cleanly shaven, though a mole near his ear was caked with blood from a morning shave.

"Silvestre Mendez. *¡Tenemos que hablar contigo. Parate!*" the man demanded in lovely singsong Spanish.

Silver figured they were undercover police and that his mother had secretly placed a call while he was in the bathroom, his face lathered from the foam of Irish Spring—he was permanently out of shaving cream. Why would she turn him in? Because of the two dollars, all in coins, he had pinched from her purse while she was making coffee? Surely not the extra-heaping bowl of shredded wheat? He slowed to a walk, his legs now like day-old mush. A fire raged in his lungs. He sucked and sucked in the winter air, but his

breath, preciously low in the sacks of his lungs, had left
him and didn't seem willing to return.

"I'm tired," Silver managed to convey to the officers.

One of the men grabbed his shoulder and dug his fingers like a clawhammer into his flesh.

"Mercy!" He buckled to his knees in the middle of
the street and in the presence of two kids eating Snickers
candy bars behind their fenced yard. Their chewing sped
up as the police raised him to his feet and led Silver to a
cruiser that had pulled up. "I ain't going nowhere!"

One of the police officers, his badge gleaming in what
was a perfect morning a minute ago, cracked, "That's what
you think."

At the police station, he was seated in a ten-by-ten
room yellow as a washed-out daffodil. The Latino officer,
a sensitive fellow, brought him two paper cups of water,
mere thimbles that wouldn't put out the fire still stoking
in his lungs.

"I don't know nothing," Silver said weakly.

The officers had briefed Silver on why he was seated
at the station and not at a table at the Cesar Chavez Library, using the U.S. college directory to hunt for names
of Latino professors to hit up for readings. On the drive,

Silver learned that his friend Al Sanchez was found dead; a tidy suicide, they explained—no blood, no puckered gunshot wound in the temple, no spillage of vomit from the mouth. Even the eyes were politely closed. His body was discovered at the wheel of his 1983 Camaro on Grizzly Peak, perched on a sandy cliff that faced the bay; the car's engine was running, and the radio was tuned to an oldies-but-goodies station. A drum kit was in the backseat. The police were baffled as to why the skins were ripped and every one of his twenty sets of drumsticks were broken like chicken bones. The destruction suggested anger. This much he was told, plus the forensic people—myopic little people in white coats—concluded that he might have died either from a stroke or a heart attack caused by numerous drugs found in his system. However, like all deaths—by murder, disease, accident, or suicide—nothing was 100 percent conclusive. Nevertheless, the coroner wrote on his clipboard: *suicide.*

"I didn't kill no one," Silver argued. His tongue was thin as a poor man's wallet because he had used so much of his bodily liquids in the foolish attempt to outpace the officers. He had also used the moisture on his panting tongue to talk the officers into letting him out on three different street corners. "Gimme me some water. I might die."

The Latino cop shook his head and sighed, apparently saddened that his Latino brother was hard of hearing.

"You're here for questioning. We're almost certain that Mr. Sanchez died from suicide. But it's good to settle matters. To know for sure, you know?"

"Al wouldn't do that."

"People do all sorts of things. Sometimes they check out just because they're tired."

Could be true, Silver mused, and turned over in his mind an image of Al dead in his car, facing the bay. In the distance stretched the Golden Gate Bridge. Under that bridge would have been a tanker heading out to sea with a load of oil sloshing in its hulls, and somewhere far below sat shirtless Koreans smoking cigarettes and playing poker by the light of a single twenty-watt bulb. Silver wondered briefly what it was like, the actual death part. A collapsing light followed by an expanding dot of blackness? He wondered how it felt to have a root growing through your head a hundred years later. He poked a finger into his ear, a semblance of a root; it didn't feel that bad.

Hitching up the hardware on his belt, the cop left when the walkie-talkie on his shoulder squawked.

The silence of the cubicle was ominous. Silver tapped the bottoms of his shoes, and hollow thuds rang against the walls. The walls, he observed as he scanned the surroundings, were like the soundboard at a radio station, a buffer between the inside and outside worlds. While not blessed with expertise in the area of acoustics, Silver supposed the walls were meant to reduce human screams once the police rolled up their sleeves and got to work. He had seen such scenes in movies, and weren't movies truer than life?

"Shit," he uttered.

His junior-high profanity bounced against the wall. The word and the nervous tapping of his shoes found no escape.

"Al, why did you do it?"

The room offered no answer.

Silver sat, head bowed, and debated twiddling his thumbs, but this unscheduled appointment with the police was serious. He had never been questioned about a suicide that could, even to a rookie cop, possibly be classified as murder by any number of high-ranking zealots. As he searched his mind, wrecked as it was at that moment, he discovered that he had never hit anyone except . . . Al Sanchez. But that was a mistake, a lucky blow of an elbow. Surely that blow of three days ago would not have made Al destroy his drums and then up and die. His body was found at night just as a young couple had parked and were ready to smooch.

"Oh, gosh," Silver moaned. "Why did you do that, Al?"

He was going to wallow in grief when two plainclothes detectives entered the room. One of them held a folder in his arms. The other held a pencil; in his hand, the pencil resembled a toothpick. The officer was huge. A dent marked his forehead, and a nick had been taken out of his ear. The officer was weathered by his job. His teeth were lug nuts in his mouth.

"Mendez," the detective with the big hands called. "We got a problem here."

"What problem is that, man?" Silver crossed his arms across his chest defiantly. He smacked his lips for moisture and was prepared to speak his mind when the detective raised a finger to his mouth and exhaled the international sign of "shut up or else." The finger was nearly as thick as Silver's wrist. His upper forearms equaled the girth of Silver's growling belly. The shredded wheat had already made a circuitous route through his upper intestines and would descend momentarily into the lower chambers. Soon his breakfast would abandon his body altogether.

"I'm Lieutenant Waldman," the detective stated. Waving his shovel-like hand in the direction of his fellow officer, he added: "And this is Sergeant Chin."

Sergeant Chin didn't look Chinese to Silver, but it was not his place to bring up race. He merely swallowed the bitter aspirin of fear.

"We have questions to ask you about Mr. Al Sanchez, who Officer Romero explained was found dead in the Oakland hills of a possible suicide," Lieutenant Waldman remarked flatly. "Is it all right with you?" He waited for an answer with his hands on his hips. His eyes roved over Silver's bony frame. The eyes passed over his arms, legs, and stomach and finally locked onto Silver's nose. With eyes pinched narrowly, the lieutenant resembled an eagle in a bad mood.

Silver had the premonition that unless he spoke up quickly, the lieutenant would extend his claw and rip off his nose, the one part of his body that he admired daily in the bathroom mirror. Without it, he would have nothing left to boast of except, perhaps, his stomach, which was flat not from gym workouts and newfangled devices but from unplanned fasting.

"I'm not under arrest, am I?" Silver asked. "I ain't done nothing."

"No, you have not been arrested," Sergeant Chin said before adding ominously, "but we know who you are."

Silver had an inkling that the sergeant referred to his poetry. After all, he had been somebody in his time—the seventies, when *el movimiento* was on the tip of every true Chicano's tongue. Perhaps somewhere along the way the detective had heard him read his poetry. Perhaps the non-Chinese-looking Sergeant Chin had been in the audience when he read at Laney College, the Oakland community college populated with Asians. Perhaps the sergeant was a sensitive book lover who, on his free days, read great and not-so-great literature in a cozy alcove, occasionally

sipping black tea in honor of his ancestors. But Silver acknowledged to himself that that probably wasn't the case;
to him, Sergeant Chin looked more like the leading student of a kung fu system called Wild Lotus Kick Ass. His
jaw was rock and, below this jutting rock, high-grade iron.
His pupils whirled with an inner fire.

Sergeant Chin flicked a finger against the folder in his
hand. "You have a tidy record, Mr. Mendez. It's mostly
loitering."

"Yeah, how come you Hispanics are always loitering?"
The lieutenant pulled rank and took over. "Your kind of
people are at every street corner from here to San Mateo.
Why the fuck is that?"

Silver envisioned the knot of gold-toothed immigrant
men standing at littered corners, their lunch the salt they
chewed from their fingernails. These men waited for some
boss man to pull up in a shiny leased truck, hook a thumb
for two or three men to consign themselves to the back,
and stutter in poor Spanish that there was work on a roof
or a weed-choked yard where ticks the color and size of
peyote buttons lay in wait. These immigrants were brown
as pennies and, to so many of the rich, mere pennies that
you walk past when you spy them on the street.

"I ain't Hispanic," Silver fired back. "I'm Chicano!"

The lieutenant laughed falsely. He reported that that
word was as dead as Mr. Sanchez, and according to him

and the U.S. census, Silver and everyone of his kind was Hispanic. It said so on government forms. "Anyhow, I don't give a shit. You got a dumb record. What kind of people loiter?"

Silver's confidence shrank. He pondered whether this overt display of rudeness was a form of police brutality.

"You were also arrested at Sanborn Park for—," the sergeant started, but was interrupted by the lieutenant, who began to laugh, the mist of a good joke fogging up his eyes. Apparently the lieutenant had done his homework and read Silver's folder. Sergeant Chin smiled, too, and procured a Kleenex from his pocket and handed it to his colleague. He continued. "You were arrested for illegal vending."

"I was just selling old record albums."

Silver recalled the day at that park on Fruitvale Avenue in the heart of Oakland's Little Mexico. With his old record albums displayed on the grass, he tried to pawn his goods onto an immigrant population who had never heard of Joe Cocker or Fleetwood Mac or even the Chicano rockers Malo. But he managed to sell a set of forks and spoons salvaged from a garbage bin and polished with his shirt-tail until they gleamed like chrome.

The sergeant read off a litany of other arrests, mainly for political demonstrations but also for passing bad checks, public drunkenness, nudity on a public beach, and defacing property.

To Silver, the last grievance was untrue.

"Nah, I wasn't defacing nothing," Silver piped up, suddenly through with being played with, for wasn't his youth honorable in its efforts to change the world? "Me and Fernie were making a mural *para la gente*. The dude hired us. The liar agreed to pay us one-fifty each and give us something special to drink."

The officers offered blank faces.

Silver reiterated, clearly this time, that he and the artist Fernie Galeano, also known as Indio because of rattles hinged onto his huaraches, were hired to do a mural on the side of a liquor store. But the store owner—recently deceased because of the forty years of tiny nips from his own wares—reneged on his word after they had painted in florid colors Che Guevara and Fidel Castro, arm in arm.

"What would you do?" Silver spoke up boldly. "Some dude hires you, even when he knows you're *puro* Chicano with your own universal ideas, and then fires your ass after you do the work? So we threw a bucket of paint on our creation. We just got probation. What's the big deal?" Silver wrapped his arms around his chest, his palms cupped in his damp armpits.

The lieutenant erected a scowl on his face and wiped it off with the back of his hand. He had to get down to business. "Let's talk about now. Your previous offenses don't seem real important right at this point in time."

Silver was prepared to argue this point, both legally and morally, but the lieutenant brought his finger to his mouth and exhaled a long, burger-scented "shissh." Silver remembered that the officer had lug nuts for teeth and shovels for hands. So his tongue, mouselike, retreated back into its dank cage.

The lieutenant reached for the folder from the sergeant, opened it up, and put on his eyeglasses, thick as tabletop glass. He paraphrased the findings, the printout held some distance from his face. "It says here you were seen fighting with the deceased, Al Sanchez, three days ago, which makes that February 19. The fight occurred at the Dip and Wash Laundromat between three and four in the afternoon. Says that you struck him and ran away with something in your hand." The lieutenant removed his glasses and inched closer to Silver. "And what exactly, Mr. Mendez, was in your hand?"

Silver allowed his arms to loosen from his chest and fall like snakes into his lap. His eyelids lowered like sails, momentarily darkening the vista of the lieutenant's pleated face. It was not necessary to search the dusty corners of his memory to clearly recall what he carried away that afternoon. His eyes fluttered open, assembled the watery figures of the detectives waiting for a reply, and closed again. In that state, he confessed, "A bra."

"A bra," the lieutenant repeated after a moment in

which he let the absurdity of this confession pass among the three of them. He pushed his meaty hand into his pocket in search of a Kleenex. He was anticipating its re-use, his eyes once again misting with the rising waters of laughter. He laughed loudly, one hand on his buddy's shoulder. His laughter slowed to sarcasm. "Now, was it a formfitting Maidenform bra or a plain ole one a gal might pick up from the half-price bin at Penney's?"

Silver knew enough not to answer. And he didn't have to open his eyes to know that the lieutenant was steaming with a shine on his forehead, nicked not from previous fights but hard-nosed interrogations. The sinews in his neck popped when he twisted his head. Slowly Silver opened his peepholes to the world. Sure enough, the officer was reddening around his gills.

"Quit playing with us, Mendez!" Lieutenant Waldman's funny bone was long gone. His anger torched the hamburger scent on his breath. He was tired of being played with.

"But that's all I had," Silver pleaded. "You see, Al attacked me and I poked him in the eye with my elbow by mistake. I tried to make him feel better by picking up his wife's bra. It was on the ground, getting dirty or ready to get dirty, I mean, because I didn't know; maybe someone was ready to step on it or something. I thought, well, maybe I'll show that I care for him and had respect for his wife. He doesn't deserve her, but what the heck—these are modern times." Silver stopped his machine-gun testimony. His attention was drawn downward to his palms, where the lines ran short, deep, and crazy.

"And where is the bra now?" the lieutenant asked.

Silver could visualize it propped like twin volcanoes on his rumpled bed. For some reason, instead of tossing it away, he stuffed it into the pocket of his army jacket and took it home.

"It's at my mom's place."

The lieutenant replaced the crumpled papers in the folder and handed it to Sergeant Chin. He rolled the pencil in his hands, the heat of such action ready to blister the yellow paint.

"That's how it is," Silver concluded, rising from his chair but sitting down when he saw a red flash in the sergeant's pupils.

"Is your mommy, maybe, wearing it at this very moment?" the lieutenant asked. His sarcasm returned. He chuckled, his smile wide enough to reveal that his gums were pink as raw meat. "Forget that question." He hitched up his pants. He acknowledged to Silver that he hadn't really been a suspect, but now, after such a wacko confession, he wasn't off the list and, in fact, might be called back for further questioning. Perhaps this death wasn't a suicide but murder. This suspicion was confirmed after the lieutenant asked if he had ever slept with the deceased's wife.

"Just a couple of times," Silver answered. "But she started it. And this was before Al and Linda were together. It was way back . . ."

The officers waited.

Silver resisted finishing his sentence. It was too hurtful, like a lattice of chicken breast bone in the throat. He and Linda—Al's wife—had known each other when they were young, taut, long-haired Chicanos who called each other "brother" and "sister," "*carnal*" and "*carnala*," as they embraced at political rallies or the dances that often followed the political rallies. And they embraced a lot, both in friendship and in sex. Back then Linda was nice on the top, a 34C, but now, as he found when he checked the label of the bra, a 38DD, a sure indication that the best years had passed and the body, like it or not, had put on weight.

When Silver began to speak from his heart, to bring back the past so the officers might understand with sympathy, Lieutenant Waldman raised a finger to his pursed lips. The story sank back to Silver's heart and stayed there after they showed him the door.

The anxiety-ridden Silver didn't immediately glance back when he exited the police station, for the frenzied hour with the two detectives still had him full of jitters. The lieutenant played with him, laughed in a manner that was more hurtful than a punch, and announced with a hearty slap on Silver's shoulder, "That's all for now. Keep outta the gutter and keep your clothes on." But if he had looked back on his escape, Silver would have noticed a three-story wing under construction—crime was boom business for the urban police, who drove cruisers with tilt steering wheels, tinted windows, and plenty of headroom to scream "shut the fuck up!" to their manacled suspects. Crime was on the rise, and so was a spanking-new addition. Cement was being poured like mush into reusable forms and a penitentiary of windows lowered from cranes and tapped snugly into place. The sparks of arc welders colored the gray days of winter. Air-generated ratchet guns blasted, and a crane whined from the roof, where it swung girders, the ribs of all tall buildings.

Silver was annoyed with himself because he had done such a poor job with his own defense in that yellow cubicle, the color of his insides. He finally wheeled around and sized up the police station, where more people were going in than coming out. The chain that raised and lowered the flag beat like a hammer against the pole. His gaze leveled to the street. Two seagulls were bickering over a dirty bagel, and a wino with no more than the oily skate of a shopping cart was sprawled on the curb. He was rolling the skate back and forth, the trajectory of truly bad times for those with no talent.

When the light winked green, Silver hurried across with two other lost souls at his side. Both were Chicanos. New in town, they asked Silver if he was familiar with the location of the recycling center. Silver was surprised by his knowledge: He told them that it was off Second Street and—good God, he knew more than he wanted to admit—it closed at four on weekdays and three on Saturdays. Each of them split off on their own private jaunt when they sighted a police officer at the end of the block. Silver braved a tour past the officer because, he reasoned brightly, what was the likelihood of being returned to the police station within minutes of one's release? Moreover, it was a curious scene. The officer was observing a woman layered in three dresses slam, then retrieve, a plastic twenty-ounce bottle of Coke.

"Charlie, what you got! Charlie, what you got! Charlie, what you want!" The woman sang her craziness.

Silver moaned at this spectacle.

The woman slammed the bottle repeatedly as if to make some point the world should know about. The officer stood with his hands on his hips, perplexed at what this illness might be called. But Silver had immediately diagnosed the illness, which surfaced in tantrums when one tried to a find a job and no boss returned your call.

Some called it frustration. Silver called it out-of-luck-and-then-some.

He put himself into gear and walked a few blocks to the farmers' market on Washington, where Linda, Al's wife, worked on Thursdays and occasionally on Sundays, the allotted days when urban and rural farmers displayed their organic crops. While it was against the law to sell nonperishable items there—CDs, radios, toys, clothes— she argued her case that the jewelry she sold was edible by chewing a four-foot necklace in front of the city council. Thus she got around the rules and even got her picture in *The Oakland Tribune*. She sold stylish macaroni necklaces and bracelets made of pumpkins seeds, plus body scents, candles, and incense sticks that you could lick for their vitamin C and cosmic content.

But Linda was nowhere to be seen. Silver splurged on a Fuji apple for forty-five cents. He chewed that fruit to its bitter core while watching a Vietnamese man with a dead cigarette in his mouth. He was shoveling ice onto bug-eyed bass, gray as the sea. Silver hankered for more than the dollar plus in coins in his pocket. He would have bought two fish and carried this surprise home to his mother, she herself a catfish with a mouth permanently pulled down in anger.

Silver parked himself on a bench. After the encounter with the police, he needed to regroup. In the shelter of his

army jacket, he didn't fear a few droplets of water, the
sustenance of life as far as he was concerned. And for him,
that bench was a pew for reflection. If only dead Al would
come to him in a dream and say, "Hey, asshole, I didn't
kill myself 'cause you got a lucky strike with your elbow.
I said adios because it was my time. See you later." Silver
needed to be released from the worry that somehow he
was responsible for Al's suicide.

Because of the rain, the farmers' market was empty
of shoppers. Even the elderly stayed away, those Houdinis
of shoplifting who would coolly pinch a grape from a
bunch and, as they pretended to wipe their hound-dog
noses or scratch their whiskered lips, deposit its globe of
sweetness into their mouths. Not only were there no
shoppers; no merchants stood behind the counters either.
The blue, tentlike awnings flapped in the wind and a few
oranges, puckered and juiceless, rolled down the street
in a sort of getaway.

Only yesterday his heart was pumping the new blood
of hope brought on by the letter from Spain, presently
tucked in his shirt pocket. He touched the front of his
shirt, as if feeling for the heart's one-two piston action,
and felt for the letter: It was still there. His heart, too,
was there, busy with its shipments of circulating blood,
but Al's motor, alas, was silenced for good.

Silver remembered his friend Felipe Cruz, who worked

as an English teacher at Hardwick College, a four-room language school on the third floor of a long-departed department store. Silver had visited Felipe off and on. His occasional visits were not to pump money from his friend—though this did often cross his mind—but to visit the storage room of the department store. The room held racks of musty, out-of-date clothes, which Silver had helped himself to. Not long ago, he was dressed in a white suit and white patent leather shoes with bronze buckles. He felt revived in that getup, like a new man. Since Silver wished others dressed in flamboyant attire, he happily informed those less fortunate than himself—writers with no books, artists with forgotten murals, musicians with broken strings and no money for replacements—of his discovery. Soon he had his imitators, six Latino John Travolta types strutting through the East Bay and snapping their fingers to the tune of "Staying Alive," the anthem of anyone who had ever had to get on his knees and crawl into a cardboard box for a rainy night.

With or without permission, Silver intended to use his friend's computer. Felipe was known as El Oso, not because of his size but the fur on his body. He was a hairy Chicano. If he had wanted to become a millionaire, Felipe could have clipped his hair and hired immigrants to weave the clippings into hairpieces. But no, Felipe became a teacher of ESL and remained hairy.

Hardwick College was in a brick building from the turn of the century. No one cared for the building, not the owner, city, or preservationists. No one paid it any mind when a weekend gardener pulled bricks from its sides and carried away a load for home projects—a planter box, a walkway, and a barbecue pit. It was a building damaged by earthquakes and fire, but a few of its rooms were rented out. When Silver arrived there in time to watch a man chip three bricks from the header over one of its windows, he stood with his hands examining the poor lettering of a handmade sign: Winter Break.

But the door was ajar. Silver climbed the steps of a stairway sputtering with nearly dead fluorescent lights, knocked on Felipe's door, and waited with his head bowed and one hand on the wall, greased with the fingerprints of foreign students. He knocked again when a chair from within squeaked. Silver pushed open the door to find Felipe slipping a pickle into his mouth. Felipe immediately raised a napkin to his mouth, offered up a polite burp, the kind a Middle Eastern prince would emit after a sumptuous meal, and greeted with his mouth full: "What's going on, Silver?"

Silver bit his lower lip, cutting a hungry stare at the debris of a deli lunch. "Hunger."

Felipe leaned back in his squeaky chair and cast his eyes on a half-eaten sandwich, his voiceless way of saying, "It's all yours."

Silver took it and peeled back the sandwich: It was his favorite, tuna with a single sheet of lettuce and a slaughtered tomato. He bit into it as he slowly lowered his bottom onto a chair wobbly as a rowboat. He chewed and swallowed thankfully his first real meal of the day. He savored his half a sandwich that would be a memory in two more lustful bites.

All the while, Felipe read the newspaper with his furry face gorged like a squirrel. He sipped through a straw of an ice-heavy Pepsi when he finished his sandwich, swabbed his teeth with his tongue, and turned to Silver. Again he asked, "What's up, Silver?"

Silver ached to divulge the story of his brief episode at the police station, but he opted to bring his old friend first the good news, then maybe disclose the bad. "I'm going to Spain."

Felipe's face worked up a grand smile. "Are you going to stay there?"

Silver laughed. "If you think you're going to get rid of me, you're wrong, Oso." He brought the letter from his shirt pocket, opened it up as carefully as a treasure map, and said, "It's from a *profesora*. I bet she's a cutie."

Felipe read the letter. His lips worked effortlessly over the Spanish, at which he was fluent, then he handed the letter back to Silver. "Sorry, but I can't lend you any money."

"I'm not here to hit on you!" Silver cried. But the possibility of a loan had entered his mind. After all, Felipe, a bear of a man, was a soft touch if stroked along the grain of his fur. "I'm here to ask you to e-mail the professor."

Felipe took the letter back from Silver. His face inches from the text, he surveyed the letter for an e-mail address in the ornate university letterhead—olgamoreno@salamanca.edu. He next asked what Silver wanted to say.

"Tell her it's a real honor to go," Silver said, his own tongue rolling over his front and back teeth, loosening the paste of his sandwich caught between the molars. "Tell her she can reach me through your address. Your Spanish is way better than mine, *qué no?*"

Felipe hooked a thumb at his burly chest. He mouthed, "My address?" He waved his hand around the office. "I'm in a professional setting, Silver. I can't let people abuse my equipment and the privilege of the use of this equipment." He held a serious face before he raised the napkin like a veil and giggled behind it.

"Ah, come on, *carnal*," Silver whined, knowing very well that his friend was pulling his leg, something he did literally in 1979 when a cop was testing his baton on Silver's head. Silver had tripped on a curb, and only Felipe saved him from a police butt whipping when he grabbed Silver's spindly leg and dragged him down the street.

"You're the only person I know who's got a computer."

Felipe constructed a steeple with his fingers. He murmured to himself and, using the heels of his shoes, rowed his swivel chair to the front of the computer, plastered with photos of his ex-students. He booted up his machine; in no time, he composed a brief note. He read it over, swiftly moved the mouse over his pad, and clicked send.

"That's it?" Silver asked in wonderment. He peered over Felipe's shoulder, dumbfounded that the message, albeit short and sweet, was being beamed to Spain and would soon be buried in the mechanical brain of another person's computer, nine time zones away. Right then, when the chance presented itself, he was going to sidle up to modern times and get an e-mail address. But first he needed an address to call home.

"What else?" Felipe asked.

"What do you mean, 'what else'?" To Silver, the question had the tone of dismissal.

"Silver, I got things to do."

"I do too."

Felipe blinked at Silver, as if wondering, "Yeah, like what?" He waited with a crushed napkin in his hand. His fingers had punched holes into the napkin, which in its present condition could be used to demonstrate some storytelling point for the Ku Klux Klan.

Silver shifted in his chair. His eyes roved in their sockets as his brain muscled up an idea. "I got to write new poems about a bud named Al. You heard about Al Sanchez, haven't you?"

Felipe shook his head and said that he didn't know any Al Sanchez. Al Rodriguez and Al Smith, but no Al Sanchez.

Silver argued that he must have heard of Al Sanchez, former member of Cambio Rama. He beat out a rhythm on his lap, a clue to the answer to this mysterious person who was going to become more mysterious once he was in the grave.

Felipe shrugged. "Never heard of the dude."

"¡Imposible! A drummer, a really good one," Silver crowed in disbelief. But he said that if Felipe read today's newspaper, he might remember the person.

"Why?"

Silver lowered his gaze into his palms, perfumed with the scent of tuna. "'Cause he's dead."

Later, as evening came on, as the meter patrol began to give up their hunt for cars parked at expired meters, a new front of clouds boiled over Oakland. Rain once again poured its same gray story onto the rich, the poor, and everyone in between. Silver fancied returning home, but who would welcome him—his mother's parrot with the vocabulary of "Hell's bells! Hell's bells!" Instead he added his two cents to the economy by purchasing a single cup of coffee at Starbucks. He hung out there all afternoon, where his mind, already jittery from the caffeine, became even more so as he reflected on Al's suicide. The police didn't express precisely how he took his life, though they made it sound like a bloodless affair. It had to be pills, Silver speculated, pills coated with the compound called bitterness. Silver searched his conscience, admitting that he had been callous with Linda—a few times in bed and adios by telephone. He dropped his head. What he gauged as a cunning departure now struck him as cowardly act.

That afternoon Silver cut short the seemingly plentiful minutes of his life by watching people bustle past the window. He enjoyed a conversation with a community college student in the dental hygiene program. He inquired about teeth, especially about the theory of daily flossing, and she asked whether poets were really loony. But mostly the two spoke of what was in their heart: the rosebushes of former lovers who, after the petals fell, all proved to be wicked thorns.

Then it was time to give up his stool at Starbucks. He pulled up his collar against the wind and rain. As he crossed the parking lot of Laney College, Silver struck his fist into his open palm, for he wanted dearly to bring home a large fish for him and his mother to devour to the comb-like spine. His mother would be weary from her job at the industrial laundry in East Oakland. Wouldn't it be nice for them—doting mother and loyal son—to share, say, a teenage shark? He would first sweep the shark with butter and herbs and squeeze lemon into its pupils like eyedrops. If I could only make her happy, he told himself.

He crossed Foothill Avenue, followed by his thin night-time shadow created by the oncoming cars. But he had nothing but rain in his shoes and poetry in his head, and the two together only made a dank broth. By the time he arrived, his army jacket had absorbed a wetness as deep as the Mediterranean Sea.

"Mom," Silver called after he kicked off his shoes in the kitchen and parked them at the entrance of the door—he was leery of tracking mud in the house. The shoes were pointed toward the door as if they were getting ready to walk out all by themselves.

His mother was on the couch in the living room. A small blanket lay on her lap. A set of knitting needles and balls of colorful yarn were crowded around her. She appeared to be the picture of fine domestic living except—"Good God!" he barked when he fully grasped the scene—she was warming her hands in the cups of Linda's bra.

Rain hung from his eyebrows. A single drop hung from

the tip of his nose. A chill brought his teeth to a chatter. He was stunned into silence by the sight of the bra. Apparently the surprises of the day were not yet over.

"Sit down, my poor son," his mother cooed in a mock attempt at sweetness. She batted her eyes and patted her lap, as if she meant for him to settle his weight in its motherly warmth. "Take off your jacket. Get comfy, dear."

Silver recognized that his mother was setting him up. She was damn sure what she held in her mitts.

"Busy day?" she asked. "More progress in meeting smart people?"

Silver shed his army jacket and, knees pressed together, positioned his bony rear end on the hassock, the brightness of the floor lamp cutting across his knees. Rain soaked, he felt as if he had been dunked in one of the industrial washers at her workplace.

"Perhaps you ran into one of your writer friends," she inquired. "And like you, my son, he was carrying an inch or two of pee in his hands." Frowning with concern, she pulled her already pulled down mouth in sadness.

"Mom, that's not fair!" He had long given up the notion of bringing home a fish to share with his mother. He wasn't even willing to open up a can of tuna for her. "Listen, I can explain."

"No, dear, it's not necessary," she protested. She pressed the bra to her cheek as if she were suffering terribly from a toothache and its cushioned warmth were salve for the pain.

"You don't know what I do!" he snapped.

"You're wrong, *mi'jo*," she countered calmly. She batted her Little Bo Peep eyelashes. "It's called nada."

Anger stiffened his spine and heated up his belly. Silver stood up, his army jacket in the crook of his arm. "You know how much it takes to do what you call nada?"

"Let me see," she replied as her gaze ventured over the living room, a trip she often took because she was always in search of a new place to clean. She finally returned to her son's face. "Nada, perhaps?"

Insulted, Silver broke away from his mother's sarcasm and disappeared to his bedroom, where he striped off his wet clothes and changed into dry pants and socks. He dried his hair on a clean T-shirt and combed its tangles with his fingers, shaped into claws that—God, yes!—would fit handsomely around his mother's throat. Through the closed door, his mother boomed, "Whose bra is this!" He wrangled from his thoughts an image of his mother pressing the bra to her own breasts, mere figs compared to the tankers Linda had apparently added to her frame. He pictured her over the furnace, the nightgown billowing about her legs, tragically veined from twenty-six years of working at an industrial laundry.

His mother stormed into the bedroom. "Answer me!

Have you been having women over?"

No women! This was the one rule of the house, that and the daily washing of his cereal bowl and spoon. He attempted to disclose why that article of lingerie was on his bed in the first place, but the words would not come out in a tidy and reasonable manner. It was like discussing what he felt when he wrote poetry or where he got his inspiration, which, for the last few years, had been the liquid muse called beer. He couldn't rouse up the energy to answer for the sudden appearance of a bra that helped contain the body of a real woman. He simply said, "It belongs to Linda."

"And who is this Linda?" she inquired while scrutinizing his bedroom, which was furnished with a bed and a chair, a mirror, a deflated soccer ball, a few posters of dead rockers, and a set of barbells that Silver could no longer lift. Monks living in the Swiss Alps owned more.

Silver sucked in some air and blew it out.

"Don't sigh at me," his mother warned. "I should be doing the sighing." Not to be outdone, she added her own sigh that was closer to a bullish snort.

When the telephone began to ring, neither of them moved. They each searched the other's face, the mother with a fierce glare and Silver with the calmness of the Dalai Lama. The standoff ended when his mother wheeled around and headed to answer the telephone in the hallway. He followed his mother's footsteps but cut into the kitchen, where his attention lighted on a bowl of fruit—bananas flecked with black spots but still edible. He could see that he had no choice but to leave. But first he would play it smart by adding a few carbohydrates to stoke the furnace inside him against the cold and the rain. His own anger could have heated him for a few blocks, but he was planning to get away as far as he could in one night. The banana would help immensely.

"It's for you," Silver's mother called in a lilting voice. "It's Linda. Our friend with the missing bra."

Silver's hand that had settled on the banana pulled away, as if its peel was juiced with electricity. Silver had been up since seven-thirty, and the day was not yet done with its fascinating turns. How did she get his number? Why was she calling him? But with such a personal article of hers in his possession, he thought, why would he *not* expect a call?

Silver took the receiver from his mother without looking at her. If he had raised the bubbles of his eyes to her face, he would have seen a grin that exposed her bridgework and two capped teeth that no solvent could clean.

"Linda?" he asked. He listened to her sniffle once and say that she had gotten his phone number from Joey, Al's brother. She began to tell Silver that Al was dead, but he stopped her to say that he already knew.

"You know?" Linda asked softly.

"I found out earlier today," Silver told her. He asked if they could talk, in private.

"When?"

Silver raised his face to his mother, who was glaring at a place on his throat. He touched his throat and examined his palm, expecting to find blood. But he discovered only a splash of rainwater, oily as salad dressing. "Right now would be great. I'll go wherever you are."

"Not tonight," she replied. But she told him that the rosary would be tomorrow and the funeral on Tuesday. She gave him the address of the funeral home, then cried that she missed Al. She added through her sobs, "And I miss you, too, Silver. I used to like you."

"You liked me?" Silver asked like a little boy. He was oblivious to his mother breathing over his shoulder.

"You know I did," she sobbed. "But that was a long time ago."

Silver swallowed. He was determined to right everything, to bring back whatever beauty she found in him. He told Linda to stay strong and that they would talk soon. He lowered the phone from his ear, pained that he had to hang up while someone was crying on the other end. He pushed past his mother, who had replaced her glare with something like a smile because *Jeopardy* was just starting. He returned to his bedroom for a dry jacket, a sweater to go below that jacket, and a hat. He couldn't locate a hat but found a wool beanie. He modeled the wool beanie in the mirror and stomped out of the room just as his mother was yelling at the television, "What is Nebraska! No! No! No! What is South Dakota! That's what I meant!"

He fueled up in the kitchen on a glass of water. He eyed the bananas quickly aging in the bowl and unhooked three from the bunch. He slipped into his wet shoes that were—for his convenience and for his mother's happiness—pointed toward the door.

The downtown bus station, home for the night, was quieter than Silver might have imagined and a restful locale to play over in his mind what Linda had told him on the telephone. Was it possible that she actually liked him? He relived the words "You know I did" and "But that was a long time ago." Could it be true? He whacked the heel of his palm against his forehead: Silver, you were such a fool!

As a poet, Silver permitted himself to lament his loss in a heavy way. He sighed for his deserted youth and pulled at the tears from his eyes. The tears soon dried, and his sighing made him out of breath. He slept, or tried to sleep, in an orange chair with a small television robbed of its dials and scrawled with hate messages that might have been composed by the White Power Idaho Boys. Still, in spite of this vista, plus the sad landscape of two sleeping places by the candy machines scrawled with equally hateful messages, he only had to occasionally feign a look at a nonexistent wristwatch to keep the security guard from ushering him out into the cold. He peered sharply at his wrist and muttered like a bad actor, "Oh, the bus is never on time! What has this world come to?" Being no one's fool, the guard was well versed in the dramatic coloring of an outright lie, all because of Silver's wool beanie, a sure sign of homelessness. The guard was familiar with Silver and other lost souls who waited for the first rubbings of daylight in order to rise and venture forth. About three in the morning, the guard waddled over, brushed the seat clean of popcorn and peanut shells, and plopped down next to Silver. They shared a bag of potato chips before each threw back his head and fell asleep, jaws open and gargling a few hours of solid sleep.

This repose, however, wrenched his body into a terrible stiffness. It caused a minor creak; he had to rotate his head and massage the back of his neck until the pain receded and he was once again good as new in the upper-body department. He yawned, stood up, and yawned once more, a mist squirting over his eyeballs. He took a baby step. He took two more as he judged the condition of his legs, rigid at first waking but finally rushing with a new shipment of blood after he circled the lobby of the bus station, now busy with arriving and departing passengers. He intended to flow with the departing passengers but not before he visited the men's room.

"Get up," he instructed his body. "*¡Andale!*" Thus he called to the cables of his muscles to transport his body over a puddle of spilled soda, scattered Cracker Jacks, and two men with wool beanies sleeping on the floor. He had seen them wander in about one in the morning and drop to one knee, then the other, and roll over like camels.

The bathroom was surprisingly clean and up-to-date with the latest in newspaper reading. Silver found a stall where he wouldn't have to worry about the germ count on the toilet seat and did his business while appraising the NBA standings as of the day before. He washed up. In the steamed-up mirror his face appeared gray, even with the dark growth on his face. He rinsed his mouth, combed his hair with his fingers, and posed at different angles. He felt revived and deduced that his recovery had much to do with his promise never to return home.

He spoke to the figure in the mirror. "Silver, you bottomed out, and now you're on the rise." This was his prophecy that morning.

From the bus station, he made his way to Hardwick College, which at that early hour was closed. He suspected as much. But when he hollered, Felipe's head appeared from a third-floor window. He had to take a doughnut from his mouth to speak.

"You got e-mail," Felipe called down to him.

Already, Silver wondered. Wasn't it just yesterday that Felipe sent the message?

"Go get some coffee," Felipe told Silver.

Silver cried poverty, patting both the front and back pockets. With that said, Felipe floated down a five-dollar bill, which the wind picked up and carried but not so far that Silver couldn't recover it with a short sprint. When money floated on the wind, Silver jumped.

This sight of an airborne greenback stirred a black brother from the bus stop bench. The brother asked, "Is that banker giving away money? I'll take some and only a little bit if he is. I ain't greedy."

Silver broke the news by saying that no, the man wasn't giving money away. "He's a friend of mine."

"I got friends, too, but they don't throw money from the window." The man snapped his fingers. "Damn, you got better amigos than me."

Silver scurried off to buy coffee, and instead of two large ones, he ordered three small ones—it's a sorry world for man or woman who wakes without coffee, Silver reflected while in line at Starbucks. When he returned, he handed the designer liquid to his new friend, whose face brightened. He bellowed a simple appreciation: "Now, that's nice!"

"A guy needs coffee, no?" asked Silver.

"You're right about that." He carefully peeled off the plastic lid and looked around for a trash bin. Finding none, he stuffed the lid into his pocket.

When Felipe buzzed him up, Silver beckoned the brother to follow.

Seeing an opening to something new, the brother jumped to, begging, "Don't go without me." He scooted alongside Silver, thanking him repeatedly for the coffee and singing "My, this is dusty but kinda nice" to the foyer of the old department store. The two climbed the stairs to the third floor, resting between landings to sip their coffee.

"I know what you need," Silver announced.

"Money?"

"No, some new clothes."

They descended to the second floor. With Silver in the lead, they made their way to the stockroom of the defunct department store.

"They got plenty of free threads," Silver claimed, his upper lip touched with a mustache of froth from his coffee. He pushed open the door whose once etched and frosted glass had been kicked in and was presently boarded up like an eye patch with cardboard. A musty smell swirled about them. "You like clothes, don't you?"

"When they free and don't say 'Oakland Jail' on the back, I do."

The two stepped into the room lit by the watery light that poured through the torn curtain.

"Who lives here? This here what they call a condominium?" the brother, whose name Silver learned was Armstrong Sender, asked. "If it is so, they got to put some order in this place." He kicked a box filled with wire hangers, which chimed like a harpsichord. He ran a thick finger across the dust on a counter. He sneezed.

"Nah, man, it ain't a condo." A tour guide, Silver explained that this was the storage room for a department store that was long gone. "Take anything you want."

"Damn," Armstrong sang. "I glad I know you!" He extended a hand, and they shook on the start of a good day. Armstrong smiled a mouthful of ruined teeth. "Ain't yet nine, and my life turn for the better. Shit, by twelve noon I might be a millionaire. Get me that house, car, and more beer than is good for you, me, or all the crazy folks we know." He giggled at this revelation, then sipped his coffee. "And I won't forget my friend. I give you a six-pack of my suds!" He giggled again. "And if I get me hold of a stove, I fix you a ham sandwich!"

While Armstrong scavenged through the piles of clothes, Silver walked up the stairs with the coffee for Felipe. The door to his office was ajar. Felipe, seated at his computer, didn't raise his attention to Silver when he knocked, entered, and placed his coffee on the table. When two minutes passed and Felipe still hadn't broken his silence, Silver asked, "What are you doing, bro?"

Felipe was grinning at the screen. His pupils were pulsating.

"You look crazy, Oso." Silver passed his hand in front of Felipe's vision. "If you are and can't eat no more, let me have a doughnut." His nose had flared and contracted when he smelled what could only be glazed doughnuts, the pastry of choice for the police and starving poets.

"Yes!" Felipe screamed. He stood up, sat back down and swiveled his chair like a merry-go-round, and settled once more in front of the computer. He punched in further commands.

After Silver had eaten two doughnuts and pounded the last drops of coffee from the bottom of his cup, Felipe told him that he was the CEO of his own destiny and was involved in on-line day trading. When he tried to outline this money venture of his, Silver said, "Huh?"

"I'm trading stocks on the Internet," Felipe said. "Got my own private hookup."

Felipe sounded as if he had tasted the trickle-down

effects of the Republican Party, but since the doughnuts were free and his cubicle threw out a bell of warmth from a heater at their feet, Silver produced a simple grin. The grin said, "I don't get it, but I want to hear more."

"I buy a stock when it goes down, even a fraction, and sell when it goes high. I strike and get out, then get in when the stock flattens. I might play for an hour or two, then sell or buy more." He flipped open a log of his transactions.

Dumbfounded at the figures, Silver admitted he was no good at math. His forte was the sensual world. He asked for another doughnut.

"I made three hundred right now with Lam Research," Felipe said.

"You're selling lambs for research? What's wrong with you, homes?"

Afraid he wasn't reaching Silver, Felipe skipped the details. "I'm saving a few bucks by living here."

Silver judged the scant surroundings but didn't see a couch, let alone a bed with two pillows, and where was the floor lamp in order to read at night? He asked if Felipe was sleeping in a chair because Silver had just done that himself at the bus station.

"Jesus!" Felipe moaned. "The bus station?"

"It wasn't bad," Silver assured Felipe. He described the friendly people who populated the station, sharing what small goods they had, even down to the last flakes of Doritos.

Felipe shook his head and poked an index finger into his ear, the rest of his fingers shaped like a handgun. He wasn't aware that his friend from the old days was this far off track. He moaned, "Good God, Silver, you're homeless."

"Nah, man, I got a home, but I don't want to go there." He pictured his mother with pins in her mouth and her nightie billowing as she stood over the floor furnace.

"Oh, Silver," Felipe cried. He handed over his own untouched coffee. Silver refused it but did claim the doughnut on a napkin. Felipe spoke of his room on the fifth floor, which he had rewired; the outlets doled out free electricity.

Silver debated whether to ask if he could stay on the floor above but quickly realized that the building was only five stories. He would be asking to stay on the roof in winter and Felipe, he feared, would either make a joke of it or start bawling, big crybaby of a bear. Also, he sensed that the time was not right to ask if he could stay with Felipe. That would come later, perhaps at midnight when the rain started pouring and he was outside meowing like a cat. He changed the subject.

"So what's my e-mail say?" Silver asked.

Felipe reached over to his desk for the printout of the

e-mail. "It says that you got to write up a brief biography about yourself."

Silver pocketed the e-mail from Felipe without reading it.

"Write it out," Felipe said. "I'm going to hit the head, then get back to work." He left with his hand reaching for his zipper.

Silver picked up an apparently depleted ballpoint pen and scratched furiously back and forth on a piece of paper. Finally, after much effort, the pen flowed red ink. He wrote that he was living in Oakland, had recently read his poetry at several community colleges, and was working on a new book, yet untitled, but leaning toward something like *Rain Poems*. He handed it to Felipe on his return from the john. Felipe read it once. His eyes rolled with confusion. "This is it?"

"That's it for now, Oso." He told Felipe that poetry was precise art and the art of poet bios was even tighter, unless, of course, you're an East Coast, brie-eating asshole poet; then you're allowed to go on for pages how you won this and that award.

Silver thanked Felipe, left his office, and went downstairs to help Armstrong break a lock off a metal cabinet. The two discovered long trench coats. They slipped them on and paraded around the storage room, the hems dragging like trains. They descended the stairs, laughing. The

two resembled characters from the movie *Superfly* when
they raised their collars and stood in the doorway of a
college that no one had heard about. Each put on his wool
beanie.

"I thank you for the clothes and coffee," Armstrong
said, squeezing Silver's shoulder. His brow became lined
with concern. "Brother, you better put on some meat."

"You can say that again." Silver noticed the white
breath of his words in the cold air.

"Here goes," Silver announced.

"Yeah, here goes whatever," Armstrong mumbled, his
beanie adjusted to his eyebrows.

The coats dragged like shadows but acted like brooms
as they gathered mud. While Armstrong went straight,
Silver skipped over three puddles to the corner, where he
pressed the button for the traffic signal to turn green, the
color of money.

Silver spent a few hours at the Cesar Chavez Library,
rooting for names of Latino professors in a massive college directory. He was amazed that most of the professors
had e-mail addresses and fax numbers in addition to telephone numbers, plus something called "voice mail." Only
a few years ago, a true Chicano writer or artist didn't have

more than a shirt or blouse to button up at the beginning of the day. How did these brothers and sisters change in ten years? Where did the street heroes go?

Silver wrote down addresses and studied a rain-speckled window behind the reference desk. Already he visualized his departure from the library when the weather would be clear, though the gutters rushed brown matter like the Ganges—twigs and leaves in the rush of water, and ants, little pilgrims in search of a dry hole, riding sticky soda cans. This departure, however, did not occur until four in the afternoon, when the security guard poked Silver awake. He warned him that sleeping was not permitted—children might get the wrong impression and fall asleep, too. The guard placed a piece of red paper in front of him: Pray With Us Rescue Center.

"It's a place to go if you need sleep," the guard suggested politely. "And I know, 'cause I been there. Showers, too, and food at six."

Silver wasn't insulted by the appraisal of his circumstance; no, he was grateful for the security guard's lax patrolling. He got to snooze twenty minutes, undisturbed except for a teething baby hollering in his stroller. And in his sleep, Linda appeared at a stove, making a hearty cheese omelet that would have satisfied a family of six. He would have to call Dr. Freud from the grave to puzzle out the dream: Did he relish a square meal and the woman to make that meal? Sleepily he ran his hands down his face and picked at the corners of his eyes. He turned to the back side of the announcement and began to compose a memorial poem for Al, using the red ballpoint pen, which made his looping script hard to read against the red paper. Still, he wrote and chopped off more minutes before he rose, donning his headdress, the wool beanie, and cleaned himself up in the public rest room. His stomach was rumbling. He hadn't eaten anything since early morning, when he devoured three doughnuts, sugary sustenance that at first made him hyper and, conversely, after the sugar burned its payload of fuel, droopy.

"Man, I could grub on a *carne asada* burrito," Silver remarked to the image of himself as he stood in front of the mirror.

"I could use one too," a voice echoed from one of the stalls.

Silver lowered his head, ostrichlike, and noted two shoes, unmatched but both resembling the heads of abused alligators. He tiptoed out of the bathroom, employing a paper towel to open the door, a safety measure against whatever muscular germs were multiplying on the door handle. He already had enough to worry about without a hoof-and-mouth disease from a public john.

From the library, he launched himself in the direction of the funeral home on High Street but stopped to watch the fire department answer a call at a senior citizens home. Old faces were pressed at the window, observing the onlookers. The breathings of these old people hardly blotted the glass, their lives having been spent. While not religious, except when in deep trouble, Silver did cross himself when the paramedics wheeled out a gurney effortlessly, the body having lost its soul. The body was draped from head to foot in a white shroud. He crossed himself again when the van pulled away without its red lights wheeling.

The apprehension of dying on a regular Thursday, in rain, dampened his heart. Too bad Al didn't get to die on Sunday, he told himself, perhaps after two fun-filled days—Friday and Saturday—of partying with friends.

When he arrived at the funeral home, the parking lot was nearly empty, though two cars were parked there: One was a gray Cadillac, property of the funeral home, and the other was Al's Camaro, now the property of Linda, Silver presumed. The driver's side of the windshield was fogged from human breathing. Silver figured that Linda had just arrived herself and was inside the faintly lit funeral home, perhaps signing forms in triplicate—one for the funeral director, one for Linda, and one for St. Peter, stuck on the night shift. But she could be sitting in prayer. In his mind's eye, he saw her applying rouge onto Al's cheeks, slightly sunken from the lack of barroom liquids, mostly beer but also tequila. Al was known to throw back shots of tequila, grimace, pound his fist in the air, and proclaim, "That's good shit," even when the shit was the blend of the cheapest grog distilled not in Mexico but an unclean warehouse in East L.A. He saw her speaking to Al as he lay in the coffin, his bejeweled hands up on his chest and ready to throw a jab. You could never tell, Silver wagered. Jesus came back looking for more of the same. Why not Al?

When Silver tried the passenger's side of the Camaro, he found it unlocked, though full of complaint as he opened it slowly. He felt like he was opening the back door of a hearse—scared, he lowered his head and got in. A shock rose like a thermometer up his spine: He was sitting where Al had died only four days before. Silver pictured Al with his head leaning forward onto the steering wheel.

"Jesus," Silver whispered. Still, he was grateful that the Camaro wasn't worth locking—crushed soda cans, burger wrappers, and a set of jumper cables lay at his feet. A statue of Jesus glowed the color of a yellow tooth on the dash. He snatched the statue off the dash and kissed the Lord's feet, which were embedded with magnets to keep Him upright—a good thing because Al was a crazy driver who often took corners with only a thumb on the steering wheel. Silver replaced Him on the dash, marveling that the statue could hang nearly perpendicular. The magnets were that strong.

Silver pulled off his wool beanie; he was surprised that his hair was a swamp of sweat. He peered out of the rain-spotted windshield as his breathing slowed and his muscles relaxed. To keep himself busy, his hands beat out the rhythm that was Al's signature sound heard from every brown puddle of a barrio from San Francisco to Chula Vista. Babies were conceived from that sound, and *vatos locos,* juiced by the power of his beat, propelled their skinny bodies against other skinny bodies. His drumming provoked the seventies to get up and dance, and if not dance, then to at least get the women against the walls to fan their pear-shaped bottoms. To pay homage, to remind himself of the master, Silver tapped a beat against his thighs but quickly tired and closed his eyes. He yawned. Sleep shrouded his mind, and soon his jaw lost its grip and fell open. A hummingbird could have drunk from the saliva that gathered at the back of his throat.

Silver was snoring the snore of an old man when the passenger's side door groaned open and Linda dropped her handbag and screamed. Silver was startled awake. For a flash of a moment, he imagined a horrible nightmare in which he was at the tail end of an accident, one in which he had fallen asleep at the wheel. He felt his head with his palm and examined that palm for a smear of blood: nothing.

"What are you doing there?" Linda asked once she made out that the person sitting in the driver's seat was Silver.

"Waiting for you," he answered groggily. He glanced toward the funeral home. "Just waiting to go in."

When Linda slid into the passenger's side of the car, Silver drew her to him and gave her a kiss just above her ear. He squeezed her again and kissed her again, and picked up the scent of soap on her skin. "I'm sorry," he said after he released her. He noticed that her forehead was lined and the skin sagged beneath her eyes, which were smudged from crying. Her eyes were red; the whites were broken up with territorial veins. He had noticed that she had put on weight, too, and her hair was gray in places. Try as he might, he couldn't wash from his mind the image of her bra, an article of clothing he had no business possessing. It floated inside his head and disappeared when she said, "I can't believe he killed himself."

Silver took her hand into his. Seeing that his hand was bony, thus comfortless, he added his second hand.

"Why would he do that?" she asked.

Silver could think of a number of reasons, but he only squeezed her hand even more. He said, "But that's what the police reported. That's what they told me."

"You talked to the cops?"

Reluctantly Silver reviewed for Linda his two hours with the police but didn't speak of his encounter with Al at the Dip and Wash Laundromat.

"That was no way to find out about a friend's death." When her eyes filled, she brought a hand up to her face to rake the tears away.

Silver wasn't sure if Al was a friend, but he was a man who made music. He could claim, however, that Linda was more than a friend, a former lover on a narrow bed in a shared apartment. His heart blossomed with something like love at the memory.

"But I don't believe he did it," Linda said. "He couldn't have."

But Silver knew Al was capable of not only taking his life but also others'. He was a madman who apparently ripped up his own drums and broke his drumsticks—or so reported the police.

They sat in silence. Rain lightly drummed on the roof of the Camaro.

"How are you, Silver?" Linda asked.

Silver wished that he could assume a British accent and cry, "Lovely, dear, just lovely." But his voice let out a meager, "Okay." When he needed strength, he had none. Only an hour ago he was dreaming of Linda in the kitchen and the high flames scuttling over a pan heavy with nine double-A eggs. Now he was tired.

"You look beat," commented Linda, touching his collar.

And at her touch, he perked up. "Oh, yeah, a little bit, but hey, I'm going to Spain." His smile, however, weakened immediately. He could feel Linda staring at his face, assessing the damage accrued over seventeen years.

"Why are you going there?" She touched his cheek with a hand hot with tears. Silver touched his own face and located the tear she left there, a seed of sorrow that might multiply on his face.

"There's a conference there on Chicano lit. And this dude's invited." He wavered whether to invite her to come along with him because he didn't wish to betray the memory of Al, bastard that he was. The time was not right.

"They have great jewelers in Toledo," she said.

Silver waited for her to say more, but she only brought a knuckle to her mouth. She bit her skin, lightly.

When the parking lot began to fill with cars, Silver told Linda that she had better go in. She ignored him. A frisking set of headlights touched her face and then returned her to darkness. "You were rotten to me."

Silver didn't need a roll call of his past deeds. He could easily remember their past when he thought of himself as a fox but was actually a weasel.

"And I liked you so much," Linda confessed. She

pulled her face from Silver and touched the cold window. She dragged a finger down the glass.

"Linda, why not now?" Silver chanced asking. "I don't have much, but I will. I'm going to write a new book of poems."

She raised her hand to his face and pinched it roughly, depositing another tear on his cheek. He almost broke down himself and cluttered up the moment with his own tears to their unlikely reunion in a dead husband's car.

Silver shook his head when she again suggested that they go somewhere after the rosary. "You should be with family. We'll see each other soon." For him, "soon" was in a day or two.

Linda left.

Silver sat in the car, and in that darkness lit only by the sweep of headlights of cars pulling into the parking lot, Silver tried to read the poem that he had written for this occasion. He could only make out every other word—*friendship, dying, voyage.* He crumpled the poem—a failed effort when courage was called for—and stuffed it in his pocket.

He got out of the car and marched through the parking lot, the dragging hem of his trench coat drinking up rainwater. He wiped his feet and plucked the wool beanie off his head. The funeral home was overwhelmed with the smell of lilacs and the scrubbed bodies of relatives, friends, former lovers, and one dead person, adjusted squarely into a bronze coffin. An elderly priest with transparent skin preached a few vague words that could have been applied to almost any corpse. Then, one by one, friends stood up and testified that Al was a good dude. Cambio Rama's one hit, "Eyeliner Baby," was played on a boom box, and afterward more prayers were said and then a line formed to view the deceased. Indeed, Al's hands were up, ready to jab and, in Silver's case, to collar him. "I knew about you and Linda! And where's that money I can't use no more?"

That night Silver stayed with Rolando and Victor Chabran, two fist-fighting brothers and former roadies of Cambio Rama. On that evening they paid homage to Al by drinking every beer in the refrigerator and going out for another case. That case, too, joined the altar of empties set next to the television, which was muted but playing a video of Woodstock. Jimi Hendrix, legs akimbo, was squirting lighter fluid on his guitar.

"Al was the best," Rolando started. "People talk shit about other drummers, but Al was a dude who could hit and not hit." He sucked on a roach, held his breath until his eyes watered, and exhaled the kind of cloud a dusty couch coughs up when spanked with a broom.

"Nah, man, I don't know what you mean," Victor slurred, egging his brother to pick up the rope of a pull-and-tug argument. Victor was younger—thirty-six to Rolando's forty-four—and sported a dark ponytail and rings in his left ear. Victor was also heavier; his belly was an old bathtub turned upside down. His jaw held a satchel of fat. His fingers were brown as hot links and would have been just as greasy if they were severed and thrown into a fry pan.

"I mean Al could be a loud ass on the drum, but also *muy suave*. Subtle, *tú sabes?* Quiet like a fly beating up a little ole bug." He thrust his hand into a tub of KFC and chose a chewed chicken bone that he placed in his mouth like a toothpick. "You know what I mean?"

"You're a drunk Mexican," Victor slurred.

Rolando's head wavered on his shoulders. "You got that right. But fuck you anyhow." His eyes narrowed into slits.

"Big brother, you make me laugh."

Rolando's head rolled drunkenly on his shoulders. "Then laugh 'cause I bought the beer."

"I don't get you."

"Get this, then, fucker." Victor blared a fart that could have scattered a pile of leaves in a gutter.

"That's a good one," Rolando slurred. "I admit it, man. I ain't got what it takes to do the same."

"Thanks, bro." When Victor stood up and hitched his pants, the satchel moved under his jaw. He sat back down as he started to totter. "I can't believe it's Al's birthday."

Rolando tilted his head and measured the meaning of what his younger brother had just uttered. It didn't register. "*¡Chale!* What the fuck do you mean?"

"I mean, asshole . . . ," Victor started, then stopped. "That's right, it ain't his birthday. *¡Chingao!* Al's dead, huh?"

Silver drew himself into his reading material, a *TV Guide* from 1986 he had uncovered from under the cushion. He ignored the brothers, who argued back and forth, and simply propelled himself out of his chair when at one in the morning they tossed the coffee table aside and started to wrestle. They knocked over the beer cans, a treasure to the homeless with shopping carts. Silver walked steadily into the kitchen and helped himself to two more KFC drumsticks and the remaining coleslaw. When he returned to the living room, Rolando, breathing hard, stabbed a finger into Silver's chest and asked roughly, "So why can't the Raiders get their shit together and win! I say it's the quarterback, and my stupid brother says it's the coach."

The two brothers glared at Silver. They demanded to

know something true before they tottered off to bed.

Silver had witnessed the brothers in fights before, most of which they won and some they lost. In either case, blood was spilled, bones crushed, mothers cussed righteously, and flaps of skin torn open and left to dry and curl like *chicharrones* on the street. Silver pursed his lips as his mind rummaged for an answer. "Good question."

"We always ask good questions," Rolando stated. A pipeline of blood flowed from his nose. "You're the poet. So what's the answer, *ese*?"

Silver was savvy in remaining neutral, for either brother was dangerous. "I think it's both situations. There's a problem with the quarterback position *and* the coach. They have to learn to work together, you know? Connect not only on the field but also off the field. They should do what you two dudes are doing for me."

"And what's that?" Rolando asked, the end of his T-shirt in his hand and ready to wipe the blood from his nose.

"Welcoming me into your house, *tu casa*. The coach should do that for his quarterback, and the quarterback if he's not an asshole should be nice, too."

The brothers squinted at each other. They nodded as the fishbowl of alcohol in their brains slowly made room for the answer. They gave each other a high five.

"Right on, *carnal!*" Victor shouted.

The two brothers exited the house, Rolando first, to throw up on a geranium that was already having a tough time surviving the winter. Rolando yakked for a full minute and spent another two cussing out the neighbor who had appeared from his house to beg the Chabran brothers to please, for the sake of the community, couldn't they hold hands and jump from the Golden Gate Bridge?

For the second night in a row, Silver slept in a chair, this one, however, a recliner with a massager that was enjoyable for ten minutes. Any longer and the action was like someone nudging you in the back with a gun over and over. And instead of facing a television with its dials gone, he was propped in front of one showing reruns of *M*A*S*H* and *Mary Tyler Moore.* He grew bored of Mary's face and punched the power on the remote control. Mary's mouth was a large bowl of teeth when the television flashed and went black.

Silver woke about ten, pleasantly rested because he had only tipped back three beers. He had feared drinking on an empty stomach and ladling his insides on the geranium, survivor of not only a hard winter but the Chabran brothers as well. He stretched, rose from the recliner, and surveyed the rubble in the living room—sour socks and shirts, girlie magazines, and the empties that lay like crushed soldiers on the floor, plus chicken drumsticks, breasts, chicken wings. The carnage of the previous night extended into the bedroom, where the two brothers lay in their underwear. Rolando had headphones on his head. His mouth was the mouth of a graveyard where the drunks and semi-drunks eventually fall.

Silver had contemplated a quick shower at the brothers' apartment, but when he pulled back the shower curtain, he found a pile of soiled clothes and brown slippers flat as run-over rats. There was also a bleach bottle, newspapers, an additional stash of girlie magazines, and a bent bicycle tire. It was a dry soup of junk that required only water and a manly stir from the plunger near the toilet to disgust every wanna-be Martha Stewart, possibly even the brothers, who were then stirring awake and already arguing about who hogged all the beer from the previous night, the effects of which they were still experiencing. The alcohol would not creep from their bodies until early afternoon. When Silver peeked into the bedroom, they appeared to be making love—two fat men wrestling for space on the plane of a dirty bed.

With the funeral at two, Silver returned on foot to Hardwick College. When he hollered from down below, his hands shaped into a trumpet, a homeless man in an orange sweater helped by hollering as well, singing and adding a few riffs of hand claps that attracted an audience and their appreciative shrapnel of nickels and dimes.

"Damn, you and me can get our act together," the brother said, pocketing the change that Silver refused. "Sing a cappella in front of movie theaters and shit." The brother raised a smile that pleated his brow. He was hopeful because he had a sandwich in his hand and it wasn't yet noon. Likewise, the extra money was a godsend.

"I already got a job," Silver lied. He relished the sandwich in the brother's hand.

"But you got a beanie on yo head," the brother observed.

Silver touched his head. Wool crowned his unwashed hair.

"Only poor people wear beanies," the brother said. "Is I right, amigo? Mexican people wear beanies too, no? Or them sombreros if you in a hot place like Fresno. Melt like butter in that place."

Silver declined to sing for his keep and jumped when the buzzer sounded. He grabbed the door and entered. Picking up the end of his trench coat, he scaled the steps in leaps.

"I need to use your shower," Silver said before he added a courteous good morning and how are you. He was breathing shallowly from the climb up.

"Where were you last night?" Felipe asked. He was seated in front of the computer.

"I went to Al's rosary."

"I waited for you. I thought you might need a place to stay." The lenses of Felipe's eyeglasses were filled with the reflection of charts and numbers from the computer screen. He was on-line day trading.

Touched by his friend's concern, Silver bellowed his thanks to Felipe and asked if he could stay the night. He pictured the two brothers stepping between the beer cans and chicken bones on the floor, stepping not lightly but heavily because the beer had drained to their legs, those huge barrels from which the rest of the body drank during the dry parts of the day. His nose then flared when he picked up the smell of fresh goods— bagels with cream cheese.

"You got e-mail," Felipe said. "I printed it out for you." He reached across his desk and brought it out from a pile of papers.

Silver took the e-mail from Felipe's desk and sat on the chair wobbly as a rowboat. His stomach made noises. To Silver, his insides were tragically toppling against the scaffold of his ribs. "Oso, do you have anything to eat?"

When Felipe didn't respond—his pen was writing figures into a log book—Silver again asked with one hand on his stomach.

Distracted, Felipe turned to Silver, the lit lenses of his eyeglasses darkening as they pulled away from the light of the computer. Silver observed that transformation and thought, Money is bright, and I'm a dark cloud. This assessment, however, didn't stop him from pushing a hand into a bag when Felipe finally replied, "We have garlic bagels."

"Calories!" Silver yelled. "That's what I need." He rifled through the bag for a bagel. He peeled back on the plastic tab of a honey container and laced his bagel with its golden sweetness.

With Felipe at the computer, Silver took his late morning treat to the hallway. At the tall window at the end of the hall, he peered out into the moving traffic on Broadway and observed the crane at the jail under construction. He chewed his chewy bagel and read the e-mail, his fist-sized heart sinking farther into its cavity of silken organs. The e-mail mentioned the participants of the spring conference—writers, poets, scholars—and Silver was reminded that two of the eleven were dead. One was a poet who hung himself in his garage in Modesto and the other, a scholar who had never gotten around to writing his book, had died of AIDS. These voices were gone.

Silver returned to get the key to Felipe's room on the fifth floor. Silver showered and lay on Felipe's couch, also a rowboat because one of its legs was broken. At every shifting, his body rocked. He remained still as a corpse as his hair dried and dreamily composed an image of Linda, who he pictured also at home, prone on a couch and wearing not much more than a scarf and the best of her edible jewelry. Her long hair was flared on a pillow. He felt no shame in his desire. Al was dead only a few days and the last crying not yet over; still, if he had it his way, he would escape with Linda to Spain. Bewitched with this image, Silver slept for a few minutes but woke when Felipe strode into the room with a fistful of computer printouts.

"*¡Lonche, carnal!*" Felipe shouted. "I got to make a call, and then we're off, homeboy." He disappeared to use the john to wash up.

Still hungry, Silver could have pulled the flesh off a live cow. He hurried downstairs and struggled through boxes of clothes to the storage room—an orange shirt with a collar wide as an elephant's ears appealed to him. He peeled off his old shirt, a blue business getup with stains under the arms. He tossed it aside and put on the orange shirt, but not before slipping on the first layer, a striped tank top. Orange shirt, tank top that showed at the throat, and black pants—a getup that would bring Oscar de La Renta crying to his knees.

"I look like a new species of bird." He wasn't sure

whether to laugh or frown, though he was cheered by the thought that his attire might have been hip for ten minutes at the end of the 1970s. He shrugged when he put on his green trench coat hemmed with mud.

The two walked three blocks to Webster Street, where a waiter short as a penguin took their names at the packed Cambodian restaurant—the city workers had gotten off twenty minutes early to clip-clop, if not spring, to the highlight of their workday, such as it was.

"We can go somewhere else," Felipe suggested.

But Silver liked what he smelled. They had to wait and watch others eat, a form of torture for Silver. More scaffolding collapsed inside his stomach. When they were finally called, Silver took off his trench coat and hung it on a bamboo rack.

"Where did you get that shirt?" Felipe asked. "Buddy boy, you look like a fashion victim."

Silver didn't bother to banter with his friend. The shirt billowed on him when they were shown a table, also a rocky affair. Silver was going to complain, but his stomach was full of noises. He ordered red curry and didn't say no to an appetizer of prawns in peanut sauce. A plate of them came before he could take two sips from his glass of water, and the five shrimp lay with their tails in the air. Silver gobbled his two and stared meanly at the fifth shrimp. He wished the penguin waiter had brought a fair share—either four or six, but now his stare gave him away.

"Go ahead," Felipe encouraged, beckoning with chopsticks.

Silver despised this offer. Still, he speared the shrimp and raked the fellow in peanut sauce. That tasty morsel from the sea lay on his tongue and then broke apart when the chewing began.

When his order of curry arrived steaming, Silver ransacked the spicy green broth for chunks of chicken. He ate hungrily. Over lunch, Silver asked his friend if he was getting rich.

"I'm doubling my money every three weeks. Something like that."

Silver craved to ask how much that added up to. If it was more than ten thousand dollars, he was going to order dessert.

"I started with a couple of thousand," Felipe whispered to Silver, who was twirling a piece of parsley between his thumb and index finger. Felipe elaborated on his financial wizardry but stopped when Silver began to turn his attention to dipping his parsley into the peanut sauce. "Never mind."

"Nah, I'm listening," Silver said. He let go of the parsley and sat up.

Felipe drank from his glass of water, wiped his hands

on a napkin, especially between his hairy fingers, and tried to get the waiter's attention.

Was Oso signaling for the dessert menu? Silver wondered. If so, the menu wouldn't come for a while since their waiter was involved in a balancing act with six plates on his arm and a foot was moving a towel back and forth. The towel was sucking up a splatter of green curry at a far table.

"So you're doing good, Oso?" Silver asked.

Felipe set down his chopsticks and eyed Silver sorrowfully. "Let me give you some money."

Silver stammered, "N-Nah, man, I'm cool," hesitated, and finally agreed that would be all right by him. He could use a boost. Hell, he could use the kind of trajectory a pilot experiences while bailing from his malfunctioning fighter jet. He peered over the table as Felipe hid his opened wallet and let his thumb enjoy the pleasure of billing out ten twenties.

"Ah, that's really good of you, Oso," Silver crowed gratefully. And he meant it. What goodness ever comes on a winter day? And he also meant it when he remarked to the waiter that the shrimp was delicious and the curry had a warm spot in his heart—the curry was sending up gases through his windpipe. "But you know," Silver commented ambitiously after the waiter placed their bill on the table, "I want to get rich like you. What if I took this money you gave me and played the stocks?" Silver's application to success hung between them.

Felipe sipped his water. Through that distorted microscopic lens of thick glass and ice cubes, his hand appeared puffy. The hair was like the eyelashes of a camel, long and thick.

"If you come up with a thousand, I'll help you. But you need that much."

Silver almost asked, "Why not *now*?" He had two hundred dollars, for Christ's sake, and by the end of the day that tidy sum would be depleted by ten or twenty dollars, depending on the amigos he came upon at the funeral. Instead he cried, "A thousand?"

"Two thousand would be better," Felipe stated.

Felipe paid and left a generous tip. They pushed their way through the door, crammed with city workers, without question the lazier bunch. At noon the workers had first dragged on cigarettes and then dragged their bodies to the cheap Oriental eateries where fans blew spicy scents on the easily pleased.

Silver arrived at St. Elizabeth's on the blast of a high-calorie lunch. But the hearse with Al's body was nowhere in sight. The few mourners milled on the sidewalk, which was warmer than within the cold medieval shadows of the church. Plus there were no tortured saints threatening them from above, just the Marlboro billboard one block away. Under the billboard, a homeless Native American brother in rubber thongs was taking inventory of his bottles and cans.

Anxious, Silver kept regarding his wrist and found not a watch but something far better than a watch—a pulse. He counted the beats and was grateful for that steady rhythm that works the body and that had managed to get him this far in life. He promised himself then and there to learn more about the body—the heart, the spleen, the kidney, the twin spongelike lungs that brought forth good air and exhaled some sort of bodily exhaust. Each day he would devote an hour or two to learning the functions of the body parts. At thirty-nine, he could spare the time to pull up a chair at the Cesar Chavez Library and brief himself on the difference between arteries and veins. And it wouldn't hurt to know why wiry hair suddenly overwhelmed his ears when he hit thirty-seven. Perhaps there was a book on that middle-age phenomenon.

Rudy Padilla, the printer who had done Silver's book, emerged from the crowd, hiked up his pants, which were already around his chest, and approached Silver. "You skinny so-and-so," Rudy greeted loudly.

Silver gasped. He was surprised how decrepit this person from the past had become, an old man when he had printed his *Tigres en Armas* and presently something beyond age. He was small as a child and gray from the ink that bled into his skin. His tie was wide as a bib, a stylish carryover from the seventies, and his shoes were white. In their heyday, those white patent leather shoes would have gotten oohs and ahs. On Rudy's feet, at the tail end of winter, one would scratch his head and ask, "Why?"

"Just like I figured," Rudy said. "Al's late for his funeral." When he laughed, coins jumbled in his pocket. In his exuberance over his joke, he danced from one foot to the other and slapped his thighs. His hearing aid popped out, and Rudy, bug-eyed, juggled the skin-colored device before it fell like an egg to the sidewalk. "*Hijole,* that would cost me three hundred if it broke." He shoved the hearing aid under Silver's nose.

"Take it away, Rudy," Silver scolded, disgusted that the thing that was nearly an internal organ almost touched his mouth.

"Hearing aids don't work unless it's in an ear," Rudy informed Silver. "You can't talk to one and expect a person to know what you're saying." He fit it back into his ear. "What did you say?"

"Nothing."

Rudy mumbled about the cold and jingled the contents

of his deep pockets. That sweet chime of coins had Silver calculating how much that sound amounted to—forty-five, fifty, fifty-five cents? Yesterday that sum would have been marvelous to possess, but with two hundred dollars warming his front pocket those coins were a pittance. He forced up a smile when Rudy said once again, this time in a near holler, that ole Al was late for his funeral and wasn't that just like him. He he he. Rudy looked around to see if others were smiling.

"So what the hell you been doing?" Rudy asked when he saw no one beaming from his joke. "I thought you was dead."

Silver was stung. He wished the old man would bleed into the background of gray clouds and what they held in their lining—gray rain that would wash into the ground.

"Nah, I'm alive and I'm going to Spain in April," Silver said. He touched his breast pocket and realized the letter was in the shirt he had shed at Hardwick College for the frilly orange one he was wearing beneath his trench coat. He would reclaim the letter later and, if gone for good, he did have her e-mail address memorized. Not all was lost.

"Is that right?" Rudy's grin revealed a set of dentures that might fit comfortably on a man—or woman—twice his size. In his mouth they seemed torturous, leftovers from a dental school in colonial times. He raised first his left hand, then his right, and together they adjusted his dentures. He clicked his tongue and smacked his lips. "That's a nice place."

"You been there?"

"No, but a buddy of mine died there."

Silver lifted his attention to a flight of geese winging effortlessly over the spire of the church. He feigned the hobby of bird watching. Maybe his appearance of indifference would send the old man away.

"He died eating bad shrimp."

Silver slowly raised a hand to the valley of his stomach, presently cooling with the hot plate of Cambodian fare. With his palm, he measured its girth and concluded the shrimp were clean, veined, and well cooked. No way he was going to succumb to death. After all, he had two hundred dollars in his pocket.

"Excuse me," Silver said to Rudy, whose hand was in his mouth, lining up the plate on his gums. He had spotted the Cadillac that carried Linda and, he assumed, Linda's parents and perhaps one or two choice relatives—Al's parents, however, were dead and not coming; they were on the arrival side. He pushed through the crowd and waited for the car to stop. When it did, a chauffeur got out in a hurry and opened the door.

Linda resembled a bride as she exited the compartment, a Kleenex held up in her hand in surrender. She wore a veil and long coat, though they were black, the color of mourning and the sky overhead. The rains had ceased, but the threat was present. Linda with her head bowed proceeded toward the church. Her brother-in-law, Joey, had his arm in her arm. Silver became jealous. To him, it was lovely to see a man and woman entering a church arm in arm, no matter the circumstance.

The hearse arrived momentarily on silent tires, the bluish exhaust scattering the wet leaves in the gutter. Although it pulled to a high curb, the mourners on the sidewalk stepped back to give the long car room to dock and shut off its engine, which shivered twice, snorted, and died with a sigh. Silver detected a possible subject for a poem in his observation. "People move away from death," he noted, and then repeated what he estimated to be a worthwhile, hell, a profound notion not on life but death. If he had a pencil, he would have written it down. He patted his front and back pockets but had neither paper nor pencil.

With this brooding thought, he climbed the steps and entered the church. He didn't wish to see the coffin rolled onto rollers that sprang from the back of the hearse and eventually heaved-ho into the arms of the pallbearers. He had seen enough.

The pews were nearly empty. The red votive candles sputtered, and the smell of melted wax hung heavily in the air. A draft slid through a stained glass window and barreled through the double door wide enough to maneuver a Cadillac. Silver realized that most people were still outside, perhaps as reluctant mourners? True, Al probably had manhandled—no, choked, slapped, beaten, and kicked like tin cans—half the people he had encountered. They had every right to linger outside or, perhaps, not to bother to show up—maybe one crony from Saturday night was at that instant soaking his sore ribs in hot bathwater laced with Epson salts. How could one have sympathy for a bully who had cracked a rib or blackened previously twenty-twenty eyeballs or angrily whacked a friend with a drumstick because he wouldn't share a joint or the backwash from a tequila bottle? Slowly, however, the bereft, the semibereft, and the obliging acquaintances filed sheepishly behind the coffin, now on a gurney and rolling up the aisle. They found their places in creaky pews.

The bronze coffin gleamed like a new penny, but where that cargo was headed was an old story: into the earth for half a million turns before his body finally fell apart and exposed him what for he was—a wind chime of bone. Nevertheless, Silver sat admiring the shiny coffin until the robed priest appeared from a room on the side of the altar and placed a framed picture of Al on top of the coffin. In the picture, Al was grinning; his front teeth—partial plates by then, the originals kicked out after a concert at the Tulare Fair—were white as Chiclets. His hair, tied in a ponytail, was long and black, and the watery gaze of his eyes showed that he had lifted a dozen or so cold brews the day before. His look was the look of a dazed man waking up from a tremendous hangover.

When the priest turned toward the pews, his robe flaring like a dress, he crossed himself, a cue for others to do the same. "It's a sad welcome."

The mourners blinked at the priest.

"We're gathered here to send off a husband, a son, a friend, and, as we all know, a musician who created a unique sound for unique people. I'm speaking of the group of which he was a part for many years—Cambio Rama." The duck-footed priest clucked this same general litany in a Spanish that was poorly accented but grammatically correct. Smirking, the priest, like a conductor, signaled with a wave of a hand for the music to begin. A rough-looking brother in a wheelchair pushed play on a boom box and the church echoed with the Chicano sound of "Eyeliner Baby."

As the song played, Silver re-created his last encounter with Al. He saw himself enter the Dip and Wash Laundromat with a bundle of clothes in his arms, the sour smell nearly gagging him. He recalled his greeting of, "Hey, Al," and Al's response of, "Hey, my ass!" Silver buried his

face in his palms, perhaps a picture of sorrow to someone across the church, say, that elderly woman rubbing lotion into her hands because it was something to
do while the priest, presently seated in a tall chair,
rubbed his hands too, although not with lotion but the
shiny oils of nervousness. No, Silver was not gorged
on sorrow. He needed to bury his face in his palms; a
complete blackness was required to explore for himself the fisticuffs at the Laundromat: Al hurling a few
good ones to his stomach and he, in return, weakly
striking Al in the eye with his elbow. Silver viewed a
flush of sparks shooting behind his lids. He saw red.
He saw himself begging Al to "let's be friends" and
"hey, the soda's on me." Shame colored his face, even
in that church, which circulated a cold wind.

"I didn't do it," he mumbled to himself. "I didn't kill
him." He pondered whether his elbow strike had caused
the fuses in Al's brain to short-circuit, flash crazily, and,
that very same day, compel him to kill himself, but not
before he turned to the backseat and demolished what he
loved best: his drum set.

The priest seemed to smirk when he said of the song,
"Wasn't that lovely?" His smirk deepened. "Let us pray."

Silver bowed his head. He recited a prayer for the
whole world—when was he going to be in a church
again?—and perked up when Linda rose gallantly from the

pew on her brother-in-law's arm. Again he felt jealous. They looked like bride and groom as they faced the mourners. Linda pulled back her veil. She was dry-eyed and calm while the brother was a spring of sorrow—tears flowed from his eyes, tinted red and small from undue suffering. Silver surmised that Joey had tossed back a few shots before the funeral and would tip back more bottles before the day was over.

"I'm happy to see you," Linda started huskily as she let go of Joey's arm and clenched her hands into fists far larger than Silver remembered. "We all knew Al. He was my husband, and he was a friend. He was drummer for a group that almost got there."

Almost got there? Silver thought. Was that what it was?

"He died because it was time."

Who says when it's time, Silver brooded. He feared that there was a time for this or that and further feared that everyone knew this except him. Was this brought up in kindergarten when he was in the back room, scrawling on the wall with red and yellow crayons?

"It was time because he had nowhere to go."

A chill ran up his spine. Nowhere to go? he alertly heeded as he sat on his hands, his body leaning toward Linda. Silver prayed that by a miracle, a small heater would appear at his feet and circle him with warmth. No, better yet, he prayed that he would soon be in Spain and seated in a patch of yellow light with a bottle of red wine at his road-scuffed boots. The wine would serve as a heater for his cold feet. But this image of Spain, sunlight, and red wine would have to wait. He was here to listen to Linda, with or without tears. Why did he ever let her go? A couple of flip-flopping moments in bed so many years ago. Then his reluctance to call her. Then his hand-over-hand fall into obscurity when the poetry stopped. He wrung his hands when she told the mourners of their years together, imperfect but that was what God had given her.

"Al and I were separated," she announced. "That's not news to most of you. You know he could be a hard guy, but he was my guy for years."

Silver gripped the pew. Why hadn't Linda told him of their separation when they were in the Camaro? He drank in every word as she described her two years alone and how she hadn't seen Al for six months since—her eyes fluttered closed to think—since she saw him sit in for an overdosed drummer in Stockton. She was selling her jewelry at a booth.

"Al died strangely." She faltered. Her gaze lifted to the tortured saints painted on the ceiling. "His drums were busted. I like to think that he was playing them, but I know that's not true. But what's true anymore?" Tears swamped her eyes, which had Silver—the poet in him was awakening—believing that he could drink from those tears and quench his thirst forever and ever. She thanked everyone for coming and then turned it over to Joey, who bawled, "Man, my brother is, like, gone! You know what I mean?"

A few nodded.

"Me and him shared a couple of cold ones just last Thursday. He loved his good times, and good times loved him." He wiped his nose with the heel of his palm. He ran his hands through his hair. "I know he got into a lotta people's faces. Maybe your face. He could be cold, you know, like angry and stuff. But if he was cold, you probably deserved it. That's how it is, and I miss the dude." He wiped his eyes, stung more from drink than lasting sorrow. "I can't believe it, man! He and I were drinking just a few days ago and now . . ."

On the wind of his testimony, even where he sat in the fifth row, Silver sniffed bourbon. And not good bourbon.

"Al was cool. He drummed for you guys, and you guys came through and bought his records. He even lent money. The guy could be touched that way, you know?"

Another chill exploded on Silver's neck and spread to his back. How much did he really owe Al? Perhaps it was more than the two hundred.

"He gave and gave, and then . . . ," Joey blubbered. "Then he killed himself because he couldn't do it no more.

You know what I mean?" A string of drool wavered from his mouth. "He's dead, man, and the only way we can see him is if we die, too. You know what I'm saying?"

Linda ushered Joey back to the pew, then returned to the altar. She asked if there were anyone who wished to say a word or two. People looked around—birds in a pew. No one moved until Rudy stood up and announced that Al was a hell of guy and always kept his promises. This prompted another needle-thin apostle from the 1970s to stand up and acknowledge his friendship with the deceased, but he also spoke of a spotty patch back in April 1976 when Al, a wild man, had pushed him against the wall and laid into him with a couple of punches. Once he was hurt, and dearly praying it was all over, Al proceeded to rifle his pockets for his stash of marijuana.

"He took a Baggie of mine that night," the man recalled. "I was mad at the dude for a long time, but I see how I was wrong. I shoulda shared."

The burial was for family and the family's closest friends. Silver was relieved because he was on foot and rued bumming a ride from Rudy Padilla to the cemetery. Perhaps his mother wasn't far off with her belittling ex-

posure—"You don't have a pot to pee in but your hands."
Over the past few days, he had reflected on her outrage at
his inability to obtain a job and narrowed his inner findings to this: He was approaching the Zen of Chicano noth-
ingness, a state that was remarkably comforting because
his only worry was his own body, rail thin but suddenly precious beyond words. To this worry, he suddenly added another: how to get to Spain with Linda,
the woman he lost so foolishly nearly two decades ago.
Her body was thick while his was thin as a tapeworm
and, in fact, possibly host to a tapeworm that had
worked itself from Mexico to Califas. But he and Linda
knew each other from *el movimiento* of the 1970s. They
could bring themselves together, pick up where Al left
off. He held not only memories of their love, but also
her bra in his bedroom. God forbid, he had no intention of ever returning home, even for Christmas.

Sheepishly, Silver followed others as they lined up to
offer their condolences. Isaac Cebolla, a onetime artist but
now a carpenter with shoulders square as the yoke of a
Chinese ox, lumbered up to Silver. He poked a finger into
Silver's arm and asked, none too quietly, for the hundred
dollars he had lent him in 1983. Since Silver was slowly
working his way toward Linda—what embarrassment if
his beloved overheard this spat!—he plunged a hand into
his pocket and brought out five twenties, two of them

reasonably clean and three that were soft as wet leaves.
He told Isaac that he had forgotten, which was no fib because 1983 was another lifetime when it came to debts.

"Sucka, I should charge you interest by smacking your
ugly face," Isaac snarled. "And I would, except I'm being
decent 'cause of Al. Al wouldn't like me smacking you
silly on the day of his funeral."

Silver wasn't sure about that. Perhaps Al would have
relished a little blood spilled on the day of his departure.

Isaac's eyes sparked and a muscle rippled on his throat
like a trout under the surface of water. Isaac stuffed the
money in his pocket, growled, "You chump," turned in
boots flecked with cement, and joined two sturdy fellows
at the end of the line.

But Silver soon cheered up when he was six steps
away from Linda. When it was Silver's turn to offer
condolences, he pressed Linda's hands into his and
muttered how his heart was heavy with sorrow for her
loss, an outright lie because he had plans that involved
her; she gathered this by how he tickled her palm with
his index finger—a slip that Mr. Freud, head shrink of
all head shrinks, would understand as plain Chicano
horniness. In reality his mind saw her with him in Spain
and seated in a patch of sunlight real as anything he
had ever dreamed before. She was smiling in this dream,
and her mouth was red from wine and his hungry kisses.

As a joke, he planned to chatter his teeth like castanets. In seriousness, he was going to part her legs and
set himself like a cello between a luxury he could only
vaguely remember. He hadn't had a woman in several
years, and his stubby tool required sharpening.

"I'll call you," he whispered. He wasn't embarrassed
by this brief fantasy. "And very soon."

Her veil was down, casting a spidery shadow across
her face. But he made out the corners of her mouth hoist-
ing up in a smile. He was buoyed by the watchful glitter
in her eye. He next directed his condolences to Joey, seated
next to her with a long face; his tears had evaporated, but
his shoulders remained slumped. They shook hands. Silver noticed that the spider tattooed near his thumb pul-
sated from circulating blood. Another such spider clung
to his throat, also pulsating.

Joey asked, "Where did you get that shirt? I used to
have one like that."

Silver parted his trench coat and allowed Joey to finger the wide lapels.

"It's like something from a long time ago," Joey remarked. "You're looking good, man. Real good."

"Thanks, man."

"Nah, thank you."

Silver conjured up a baffled face.

"Al said he saw you just before he died." Joey waited.

A fat tear rolled heavily from his left eye, and the spider tattoo on his thumb began to pop up and down as Joey's breathing became shallow. "What did my brother say to you?"

Silver raised his beatific stare to the tall ceramic St. Francis, hollow at the center but meaningful for the lovers of birds, rabbits, and wet-nosed deer. He lowered his gaze onto Joey. "He said that he loved life, his music, and family." Right then Silver realized the power of saints and admonished himself for thinking badly of the priest who presided over the service. It took every sinew in his throat to lie to Joey. Silver imagined the strength it took to fabricate the Christian afterlife. The priest in his swishing robe moved boulders with his lying tongue.

Silver fled the church just as an armada of clouds parted and a strip of blue showed itself—it was February, but spring was around the corner! But when he rounded the corner that hailed the Marlboro billboard, he found not daffodils opening up but the Indian brother he had seen earlier taking inventory of his stock of cans and bottles. Seated on an industrial-sized soy sauce canister, he was eating a sandwich, thin on meat but bolstered by tomato and sprouts. The Indian brother's eyes were milky with cataracts. He was through seeing the world clearly.

"Looks good," Silver said, unable to walk past this man without a greeting. There was mayonnaise on the brother's chin.

"Hippie sandwich," the brother remarked. He pulled at the threads of the sprouts. "It scrubs out the stomach. Better than fasting." He pointed to a deli. "They got day-old ones if you ask real nice or real mean, but nothing in between."

Silver's hair fluttered in the wind. His arms felt weak, like cables brought down by a storm and hanging limply from his shoulders. He asked the Indian brother, "Which were you today?"

The Indian brother had discovered the mayonnaise on his chin. He touched it with a finger and brought that dollop to his mouth. His eyes were ruined but his smile complete. "I was nice. Said I would die soon and they don't have to worry about for food when I'm gone. I said they can sell all their sandwiches, even the stale ones." With this, he took a bite and began to chew.

Before Silver could wheel around to hide his sorrow, tears blurred his eyesight. He was staggered by this man in plaid pants and rubber thongs, a natural being so far from his prairie that he was never going to get back. Silver dug into his pants pockets and pulled out two of the five twenties and pressed them into the Indian brother's hand, greased from his late afternoon meal. Since he owed debts, why not pay it out now?

Silver scampered away with no earth to stamp a trail,

just hard concrete and black asphalt. Instead of returning to Hardwick College, his comfy sanctuary where he could read magazines until bedtime, he circled the streets with moist eyes. Later, as evening in downtown Oakland lapsed into darkness, he found a chair to sleep in at the bus station. All night, he admonished himself for not paying out to the Indian brother all that he carried.

The morning sky was dull as nickel, flat, too, in spite of the view of the Oakland skyline. Flat is how it appeared and how it would remain. Silver measured the day from where he lounged groggily in his orange chair, his wool beanie stuffed in the hole of one of the TV dials gutted long ago. He pulled it out, dusted it with three slaps against his forearm, and fitted it onto his head. His eyes were watery from a poor sleep; he used a little splash of that nightly runoff to clear the crust from the corners of his eyes. He got up stiffly, his backbone ossified from sitting up all night. Instead of using the facilities at the bus station, Silver tramped back to Hardwick College, where he hollered like a cat to be let in.

Felipe's head appeared from the third-story window. From that height, his head was small and dark, hairy as a ball of yarn. "I'm glad you're here. I need your help."

Silver liked the ring of that urgency and brightened up. When Felipe buzzed him up, he sprinted up the steps. But as he approached Felipe's office, he told himself that he should keep mum regarding where he spent the evening. It might depress Felipe to know that he slept once more at the bus station.

"So what's up?" Silver asked. He scanned Felipe's office for a box of out-of-date books to move or perhaps a piece of ancient business machinery, such as a boulder-sized typewriter. He scanned the room for a broom, believing it was time to whack at the herds of dust that grazed under the desk and behind the bookshelf.

"I got a call from a student." A young woman named Mariko Ono or Mariko Uno had just gotten off a flight on Japan Airlines the day before and wanted to start English conversation classes—*pronto*. She was gung ho and offering money, he explained, both hands busily scratching his belly. "Where were you last night? I waited up."

"I stayed at a friend's house." Silver pictured the waiting room of the bus station. He pictured the Mexicano who snored with a roped carton in his lap.

"I'm real busy, Silver. If you can, help me out, man." The computer held colorful pie charts of the financials for the day.

Silver found his morning call. He hurried away to

shower and shave, then picked like a crow from the pile of clothes in the storage room. He scrounged another orange shirt with wide lapels but opted for a stately wardrobe in order to tutor English: a pin-striped shirt and a blue blazer tight around the armpits but with an impressive coat of arms on the breast pocket. He also found a green clip-on tie.

Thus dressed, Silver helped a young Japanese woman with her English, tattered with misused verbs but clearly on the right track when she uttered, "Give me a break."

"Real good, girl," Silver chimed. "Try it again, but with *corazón*." He pounded his heart for emphasis.

She pounded her own heart and preached, "Give me a break, *corazón*," sounding like the teenager she was. Silver learned that she was nineteen and a former sales employee who used to greet customers at an escalator at a fancy department store.

He proceeded to teach her "Simón, *ese!*" Silver slapped his thigh giddily when she gave it a try. "You're all right, girl."

"You're all right, girl." Mariko giggled with her hand in front of her teeth. "Simón, *ese!*"

Silver toyed with the idea of building up her vocabulary with additional Chicano phrases, but he fell back to more common expressions, though he did teach her, "Get out of my face," a helpful phrase if she intended to ride

BART after ten at night.

After two hours, she rose and bowed to him not once but twice. She offered him an apple from her Hello Kitty backpack. She had carried it from Japan to present to her first teacher. She had heard that teachers in America liked apples.

Tears nearly flowed from Silver's eyes at this sweetness. Would his crying ever end?

"You good teacher, *corazón*," she said with a giggle. She presented him with a small envelope trimmed in gold and tied with a ribbon. She promised to return once the spring session started.

Silver almost employed his nostril to sniff for perfume, but he checked himself. "Is it a note from your mom or something?"

When Mariko shook her head, her unevenly cut bangs became wild with motion. "It is money." Her purse was on her shoulders. A single key—YMCA? a youth hostel?— shone in her hands like nail clippers. She repeated: "You good teacher. I like simón, *ese!*"

Silver would have shoved the envelope back into her hands, but he feared that such an action on his part would shame her or him. He intended to explore Japanese etiquette at a later time.

"It was a lot of fun," Silver said honestly, aching to hug this young woman, who was already in the doorway.

After her departure—a flower on a gray day—he was left with an apple, bruised in one place but shiny no matter how he rotated it in his hands. He undid his tie and the top button of his shirt. He opened the envelope carefully and fingered a twenty-dollar bill crisp as the collar of his shirt. With that money, he went out and bought two coffees plus bagels with cream cheese. He bought himself a packet of disposable razors and a comb and a roll of breath mints.

He returned with his purchases and shared the coffee and bagels with Felipe. He handed over one of the razors, confessing that he had swiped one from Felipe's makeshift medicine cabinet of a cardboard box. He dragged a chair next to Felipe and watched in silence as his friend commanded the computer. Silver was aghast at the chart of dollars that showed the lows and highs for the day.

"Are you really rich, Oso?" Silver asked directly, not wanting to fool around. He was prepared to whistle at the zeros that might add up to a million. The whistling would have to wait.

"In my dreams."

"How much do you got, then? I won't tell anyone."

Felipe shook his head. "If you want to play the market, you gotta come up with two thousand. *¿Recuerdas?*" He took up the water bottle on his desk and squirted a stream of yellow liquid into his mouth.

"What are you drinking?" Silver inquired.

"A Mayan herbal tea called chacawui." He told an obliging Silver to open his mouth and gave him a long blast while describing the value of the drink. Felipe touted its mineral properties as cleansers, rejuvenators, stabilizers, and basic lifesavers for computer hacks such as himself trapped eight hours a day in the toxic environments of corporate America. The tea was an earth power; goats were known to nibble its leaves and leap over streams and lakes. The Mayans themselves could drink an ounce or two and run on moonless nights without tripping over snakes and spiky reptiles. And mind you, they could work their corn from sunrise to sunset and make love to their women while lying on their backs and puzzling over the cosmic nature of stars. The tea did everything, including untwist twisted-up bowels and clear up the leprous spread of teenage acne. Plus if you bought a dozen ten-ounce packages of the mix, the company sent along a colon cleanser free of charge.

Silver set the bottle of crud down and wiped his tongue on his lapel. "Tastes nasty!"

"It's the nasty stuff that's good." Felipe unscrewed the top of the water bottle; Silver, one eye winking, peered in: He saw a yellow sediment and an object that resembled a dead tadpole.

Disgusted, Silver hung out his tongue, a short platform of semipink flesh. "I just drank that shit?"

Felipe's giggling moved the rolls of hairy fat under his shirt. He got back on the computer while Silver observed in silence, his knees pressed together. He didn't have to reach down to his pocket and pat the remaining dollars bills stuffed there. "Do I have any e-mail?"

Felipe shook his head and drew his hands away from the keyboard. His shoulders fell. He inquired tastefully about the funeral service because after Silver had left, he remembered Al Sanchez. "He tried to kick my ass at a Christmas party."

"Yeah, that's Al," Silver mumbled. He constructed in his mind an ugly scene of Al throwing a few tidy shots to the spleen and following up with a little piston action to the jaw. He saw Al bear-hug Felipe until his breath was gone, then toss him aside for one of the Chabran brothers to pick up where Al left off. But he'd had enough of Al for the day. He remembered why he was there, with Felipe. "Oso, you think I can get rich like in a month or maybe even in a couple of weeks? Spain is calling."

Felipe had his doubts and told him so. Unless he could come up with a couple of thousand, he had better just think of going to Los Angeles, which wasn't Spain but a great place to practice Spanish. Felipe knew of a restaurant where they served killer tapas. Wasn't that enough of an adventure?

"Nah, I want to go to Spain, man. I want to go with Linda!"

"Who's Linda?" Felipe asked.

"The wife of the guy who died. Al."

Felipe's mouth fell open. Knowing where Silver was headed, he reached for his water bottle, shook its contents, and began to squeeze the mixture into his mouth.

"She's the one I want to go with," Silver said.

This announcement was no surprise to Felipe. He choked the water bottle, forcing the mixture down his throat.

"I mean, his ex-wife. You know they didn't live together for a long—" His chatter stopped in midsentence. He sat in awe of a friend who could drink such a concoction without passing out.

"It just don't seem right." Felipe sounded like an out-of-breath swimmer. He wiped his mouth with the back of his hand. "Didn't this guy just die?"

"Yeah, but I'm in love, Oso."

"Jesus!" Felipe cried with worry. "I think you're going to need some of this."

Silver eyed the water bottle and then Felipe's hand that rose up and latched onto the back of his neck. There was no escape. Silver reluctantly opened his mouth and

Felipe let lose a squirt that nearly drowned him on the third floor of a building the city fathers were planning to condemn.

That night, Silver wiggled his bones into a sleeping bag and in the dark relished naughty thoughts of Linda, who he positioned on a large bed, her legs fanning in and out, an action that provided the scented breeze of a woman on fire. He touched his mouth: A wet smile lay across his face. His hand wandered into his underwear: His member was not completely stiff but stiff enough to nudge a door closed with a single wag. The next morning, he woke before Felipe, a bear with blankets up over his head.

"I'm going to use the phone," he said.

Felipe snored.

Silver tiptoed to Felipe's office. He called Linda, the telephone in both hands as if the weight of his words were iron. He had never made a call to profess love, especially right after a funeral. But he had given her, he figured, a day to recover.

"Hello? Linda?" Silver asked when a voice answered. The voice belonged to Linda, but he was surprised by her chipper response of, "Oh, hi, Silver." The greeting was almost too friendly. Had she quickly tallied her losses of her no-good husband and moved on? He stalled, then started after he choked down a dry bone of nervousness. "How are you doing today?" A lame question, he realized. She might sound chipper, but perhaps she was masking her sadness. Tears were probably still on her cheeks, and the forecast for the day predicted dark shadows under her puffy eyes. How did he expect her to feel at eight twenty-two on a cold morning, some forty-one hours since the bronze casket of her hubby was lowered into the ground?

"I'm okay," Linda replied, her voice now flat. "I feel relieved. It's over."

Silver wasn't sure what she meant by "relieved" but was familiar with the many-layered meaning of "it's over," a phrase that had been used on him in at least three different languages—Lupita, Kimiko, and foul-mouthed Mary Lou from Bakersfield came to mind. He risked everything by asking if she would like to go out for coffee.

"I can't," she said. Then she added: "Were you fingering my palm at the funeral?"

Silver jumped. His hand pulled nervously at his hair. She did feel his come-on, a stroke of his index finger in the delta of her creased palm. "Well, a little bit," he confessed boyishly. He decided not to ask if she had enjoyed that tickle.

Linda laughed. "Silver, you're naughty."

Silver admitted as much. And Linda admitted that she would like to see him. "Tomorrow, if you have time."

Silver had more time than the sky had rain. They settled on meeting at nine at the Starbucks on Broadway. They could warm up their stomachs on coffee and a roll or go somewhere else if she preferred.

"You feel okay?" Silver risked repeating.

"I feel okay." Her voice had flattened even further.

"You sure?"

"I'm sure. Look, I gotta go, Silver." She had to sift through Al's things and that would take a day, possibly longer but maybe less because Joey wanted everything—his records and CDs, his clothes, his knife and dagger collection, his second drum kit. There were also scrapbooks in the garage. She thanked him for calling, then hung up.

"She wants to see me!" Silver bragged with no one around.

Back upstairs, he found Felipe sitting on the edge of his bed, rubbing his face. Felipe, hairy as he was, didn't usually sleep in pajamas. He often didn't sleep in underwear either, but out of courtesy for Silver, his guest, he pulled on boxers with red hearts.

"I got a date with Linda!" Silver rejoiced.

"Jesus, help us. Solve our indiscretions." Felipe stood up, sat back down, and climbed back into bed, grumbling because usually at seven he was seated at the computer.

"Look at me," he moaned sickly. "In bed losing money."
He complained that he was both tired *and* worried, a combination that no quaffing of chacawui tea could remedy by noon. He retold the story of ole Al planting a couple of punches into his gut. He sat up. "Doesn't Al have a brother?"

"Yeah, his name is Joey."

"Oh, Jesus! *¡Santa María!*" With this insight, he fell back into bed, rolled over, and feigned sleep, although his eyelids twitched. Silver climbed into his sleeping bag and feigned sleep, too, hoping to turn over in his mind a few images of Linda, bare chested in front of a mirror, thus amplifying what he knew was already a huge gift for a skinny man. But he only tossed a few times and got up when Felipe kicked back his blankets and wailed, "Jesus! *¡Santa María!* Let the stock market dive, but let me live!"

"That's not how I feel," Silver crowed. "I feel good."
He roared from his sleeping bag and showered until his skin hurt from the blast of hot water and a scrubbing that could have blistered paint from wood.

That morning they drank coffee and ate breakfast burritos from Taco Bell. Felipe did his best to instruct Silver how on-line day trading worked, but not before stirring up a new batch of potable chacawui. He chugged it down; a sediment of yellow ringed his mouth like a clown.

"You got stuff around your *boca*," Silver said, offering a paper napkin.

Felipe accepted the napkin and dabbed his mouth. He studied the napkin. "Yeah, but I'm glad it ain't blood." He shook his head at Silver. "I can't believe that you're going to go out with a woman whose husband just died."

"Have you heard of love?"

"Yeah, but I also heard of knife wounds and death by drowning." Felipe warned Silver that the Sanchez family were all unruly as pirates. He had better watch his step.

Silver didn't lose hope, even when he didn't understand a word Felipe professed about on-line day trading. No, he was floating on the highest drug of all: middle-aged love. He left Felipe to day-trade and went downstairs when he remembered the letter from Profesora Moreno that he had in his old shirt, which he spotted easily from the spread of stains under its arms. He located another new shirt for the day. He returned upstairs and instead of bothering Felipe, he took a *Newsweek* magazine out into the hallway, where he placed a chair near the window. He let the *Newsweek* slip from his hands. What news could he gather from a year-old magazine when he had a bird's-eye view of Broadway Avenue, the main artery of Oakland, a city that had yet to decide whether to climb out of its economic hole or simply pitch its tent down below in its dregs and yell, "Fuck it!"

Cars crawled on Broadway, none of them tooting, for what was the hurry? A few of the city workers were running with umbrellas, though the rain fell no harder than a light tap from a leaky faucet. A postman was wiggling a key into a blue mailbox, his pith helmet an awning against the rumor of hail. Stray dogs with bent tails poked their noses in doorways in search of tidbits of sandwich and burritos. An officer—perhaps the Latino cop with the scrubbed face—was nudging a poor guy on a bench to get the hell out of the cold. The poor guy's wool beanie was nearly pulled down to his nose. Silver observed this bustle from the fifth floor.

That afternoon Silver and Felipe went out for a cheap lunch of Chinese sweet and sour, a couple of pork buns, and a pot of black tea that swirled in their stomachs all the way back to Hardwick College. Felipe got back to his computer, while Silver bided his time reworking the poem for Al, which he had failed to read at the rosary. As he sat cross-legged, he didn't know what he meant by the line "Death is a black horse with glue for eyes." But it meant something a few nights ago and might mean something later, especially if, by chance, he encountered a horse and examined its lids for a deposit of gluey substance.

Silver grew tired of the poem, a wet yawn ending their friendship. He shrugged into his coat, left the building, and walked up and down Washington Street, where Linda,

on sunnier days, would have been selling her jewelry under a blue awning. There he ran into Armstrong, the
brother with the identical trench coat. Only three days
old, and the coat was muddier than if he had frolicked
with ducks on a chewed-up lawn.

"My man!" the brother sang.

Silver let the man hug him, and the smell of
homelessness stayed on Silver after the embrace broke
apart. Armstrong reported what he had eaten during the
last two days—plenty of Chinese noodles, a giveaway from
the merchants on Webster Street, plus some ribs and at
least three burgers. He boasted that he had earned two
dollars by helping push-start a car, although his sock got
wet when his shoe kicked off in the process and a meter
maid gleefully ran over it on purpose. Each warned the
other about the police, quick on the trigger because
through the fog and rain they thought that they were invisible ninjas and had the freedom to raise their clubs freely
on the poor and unemployed. Silver had told Armstrong
about the cubicle that he sat in four days before.

Armstrong snapped his fingers. "I been there. They
call it the 'house.' They got these walls with little holes."
His thumb and index finger came together, indicating the
sizes of the holes.

"It's so people won't hear you screaming if they beat
you."

"Or laugh," Armstrong said. "I crack up sometimes when people hit me. Crazy shit, huh?"

They parted, both of them laughing. Both were being whipped by street life. Silver knew there was a poem there, but one poem for the day was enough.

Silver backtracked to Hardwick College, let himself in with a key that Felipe had given him, and climbed the stairs to the fifth floor, their bedroom. He slept with a pencil in his hand and a sheet of paper by his ear—he wanted to prove that he could write two poems in a day, but the pulleys on his eyelids broke and his mind tumbled into blackness.

That night he and Felipe went to see *Central Station* at a flea-battling movie house in Berkeley. Silver set aside his popcorn and abandoned the last watery slurps of his soda. The movie was disturbing. He gushed enough tears to float a matchstick from Oakland to Modesto when the boy, an unwanted street urchin, curled up in the littered train station and slept the sleep of orphans, one eye open. The boy slept with his hands curled around the salt of a long day. Wasn't this him at the bus station?

The next morning, Silver was up before dawn. He showered long and hard and splashed his neck and his chest with Brut, the brisk cologne that not only scented a man but also acted as an antiseptic for cuts and wounds. However, he washed his throat to rid himself of the overwhelming scent—he didn't want to be obvious. His manner was to play it cool, be suave, another Julio Iglesias unleashed upon the world.

"I'm going," Silver told Felipe.

Felipe snored, his blankets kicked off. His chest was so hairy, he resembled the werewolf in midtransformation into his full canine status.

"You're all right, Oso," Silver whispered. What other friend would take him? What friend would offer bagels, burritos, and pork buns, plus money? He touched his front pants pocket, where he kept his bills. He touched his shirt pocket, where he kept the letter from Spain. Both had value.

The night had rained, howled, and stripped trees of even their bark. The sky hardened to cement gray, though the gutters ran with water, twigs, and an occasional coffee cup smeared with lipstick. Silver spotted one of those coffee cups touched with red lipstick and visualized Linda's mouth on his throat, her teeth gratefully nibbling his flesh.

He gave himself a five-word speech: "For Pete's sake, calm down!" His breath hung before him as he walked in the direction of Starbucks, a place for the lonely to hang their sadness—after all, a person could only drink so much coffee. With the walk only three minutes long, he arrived early, even after the exercise of bending down and double tying his shoelaces. He peered into the window: Linda wasn't there. Seeing that he still had fifteen minutes, he strolled in the direction of a lake that had gathered in a vacant lot. In this body of water sailed two geese clacking bills shaped like shoehorns—couldn't asshole man, he cursed silently, offer a better preserve for these birds from Canada? After all, they did fly five thousand miles, and for what? To swim in the yellowish water that floated beer cans, potato chip bags, and blown condoms? To pull up bottle caps from the three-inch depth of muck that the sun would burn off by April?

"Jesus, help them," Silver begged. "For God's sake, make 'em fly away."

Silver hankered to gather the geese in his arms and toss them into the air; instead he ran away, none too proud of his actions, for he could have at least said a prayer for those little creatures that didn't seem to know better. The day was not starting as he believed it should, meaning the progression of brushing one's teeth and moving toward a cathartic blossom of beauty. He realized, however, it was too early to tell. For Christ's sake, it was only three minutes before nine. He tried to regroup. He imagined a decent world of love and peace where the giraffe played badminton with the lion and the raccoon dealt a fair hand of poker to the hamster.

Silver sighed as he shuffled his shoes in the other

direction and headed back toward Starbucks. When he arrived with his hands in his trench coat—a nice touch, pure poetry, etc.—his heart leapt with joy when he spied Linda. While her eyes were hooded from a poor sleep, there was blush on her cheeks, a clear sign to Silver that she must have fiddled with her appearance in a mirror. He instructed himself, Be cool, *ese*. This is just the beginning.

But he couldn't help himself. "Linda!" he called loudly. His legs, "getaway sticks" he often called them, propelled him in hurried but awkward steps. "Linda! I was waiting earlier! I went to go see the geese! But I was waiting, really!"

Silver admonished his legs and lips, two independent appendages, but had high regard for his hands when they instinctively took her by the arms. She didn't pull away even after he said, "I want to be with you."

Linda smiled and stepped back, but not powerfully.

"For a long time," he added. "What do you think of Spain? It's not raining over there."

They drank coffee and shared a large bun freckled with seeds. Silver spoke directly, for he had opened up his veins—so to speak—and he had not much time to bleed until his heart ran water and, perhaps, a little pus from some infection from the past. He confessed he was a lost soul. Now he wanted to be with her and—a long sip from his cooled coffee—to take her to Spain.

Linda spanked his wrist. "You're silly."

Silver acknowledged this portrait and remained confident when she called him unrealistic. Silver compounded his troubles by informing Linda that he didn't have much money, in fact, almost none, now down to less than a hundred dollars. He shrugged, but he had a dream that he could cash out. He told her how he pictured the two of them sitting in sunlight with a bottle of Spanish red wine at their feet.

Linda smiled. Her teeth were small and white in her broad face. "What kind of wine?"

"What kind of wine?" Silver asked, his brow furrowed and his lips pursed and ready to toot a whistle to cover up his ignorance. Over the years he had drunk what was placed in front of him, but he seldom paid any mind to the label, let alone the quality, his concern limited to the amount that remained in the bottle. His purpose was to reach a buzz and stay afloat until bedtime. "Well, the kind that's like the grapy taste of the last days of summer and after a period of aging—usually two weeks—is poured into the goblets of true love." He conceded that he was blasting away on the trumpet of bullshit, but that was him, the poet inside coming out. He almost laughed when he told her he had once got drunk on the sweaty nectar of grape-stomping virgins.. . .

"Be quiet! You don't know wines." Linda laughed and covered up her teeth with a napkin. Crablike, her hands crawled over his. "Silver, you weren't very nice to me back when." Her smile flattened. What brightness had played on her face now vanished. Yet her hand remained over his.

Silver couldn't shrug off this piece of history. He had gone to bed with her four times, perhaps five, but he tired of the routine of showering and gassing up his car, then a Volkswagen with Chicano Power! painted on the driver's side, and fighting traffic all the way to Hayward, where she lived with her mother at the time. He hadn't called her until seventeen years later. By then her husband was buried and—good God—tucked snugly into his grave not more than three days. His bones were just getting comfy.

"Yeah, I know," he repented flatly. The brightness on his own face passed and was replaced with shadow.

"Why now?" Linda asked. Her hand pulled away from Silver's hand.

"Can we talk about wine?" Silver asked playfully. He believed that she might laugh, but he was wrong. Linda's eyes could have burned a hole through him or, at least, reheated his coffee. She glanced over Silver's shoulder at a couple at another table, their hands laced together. She jerked her chin at them. "That was us for a couple of days."

"That's us right now, Linda." Silver was surprised by his strength.

She turned back to him and placed her hand over Silver's. "Look, Al just died."

"Al died a long time ago." He wasn't sure what he meant by this, but it was a sentence to distribute between them. It felt forceful. "We died, too, but I think we can come back." He was less confident with this line, but he noticed that Linda didn't fight that vague allusion to a resurrection. He advanced after two quick sips of coffee. He chided himself for his youth and stupidity but confessed that if he could call back the years, he would do nothing different.

"Screw me and leave?" Her hand pulled away.

"Yeah. Because I was nowhere. I was failing. Because in the end I'm going to have you. Because I'm going somewhere now." Silver understood this clearly. He was a popular poet for five years, and then the invitations to sit on panels and do poetry readings stopped. One day he was famous, and the next day he was counting his change in an ashtray.

Linda stared at the crumbs of their shared bun. She saw that her fingernails were packed with crumbs. "You and Al. Al with his drums and you with your poetry. Your

Chicano thing!"

"Baby, we were doing what was natural back then."

"Yeah, on a lot of women. I don't know what kids he had without me. Or you, either! How many do you have?"

Silver let that slide off him. He eyed the clock and waited for its long hand to rake another minute from the day. He gave her this much time to manage her anger.

"We're going to sell the Camaro," Silver said. "We're going to sell it, and I'm going to take the money and trade on line."

Linda tilted her head, confused.

Silver told her about Felipe and on-line day trading. "We sell the car and double our money."

"I don't know what you're talking about. Do you?"

"It's the only way," he said. Again his meaning was lost not only on Linda but also on himself. He sipped the coffee that trembled in his shaky grip. He admitted that he didn't know beans about on-line day trading. But his friend's touch was gold, and he trusted him with everything he owned, the meager collateral of future poems.

Linda dug at the crumbs, now paste, under her fingernails. "Silver, look at me."

He did what she asked.

"I'm big and fat." She hesitated but added, "And almost old."

He stood up, scooting away his chair, and undid the

buttons and belt of his trench coat. "Girl, I'm nothing but bone. I've known dogs with more meat to them." Silver felt naked when Linda's stare fell from his face to his crotch. "What are you thinking?" He quickly closed his coat and roped it with the belt. He sensed she was sizing up his tool.

"Never mind," she scolded mildly. Her smile returned.

He smiled, said it was time to go, and took her arm, leading her away from the table. But she stopped him. "I have to use the rest room." Her hands crawled from the crook of his arm to his shoulder. "Do you really want this?"

"I want you."

"I don't think you know what you want, Silver."

Silver shook his head and told her she was wrong. In the breeze of his head shake, he could smell the Brut on his skin and was grateful for that whiff, which suggested both romance and sound hygiene. Certainly Linda had picked up its lovely scent and likely his change in character?

While Linda was in the rest room, Silver spied the young couple. They *did* look like them, except when the girl spoke, she had a chrome ball latched on her tongue. The young man sported a ring in his eyebrow and one in his nose. He could see they were in love. Their napkins were shredded from nervousness. He looked back at the table where he and Linda sat: His own napkin was balled up, but if he had shaken it, the napkin pieces would have rained down like confetti.

When Linda reappeared, rubbing lotion into her hands, Silver took her arm and they exited Starbucks, a stock not worth buying, he deduced in wise fashion, because it was high, not low, and what they were searching for were stocks that were trampled on. He acquainted her with his gut findings.

"Like us?" Linda asked.

Silver hesitated. "Yeah, like us."

The sky was gray, though marked with an impressive chevron of migrating geese. They walked arm in arm to the end of the block, and Linda pulled on Silver to slow him to a stop. She pointed at the street where she sold jewelry. She brought a necklace from under her sweater. "See what I made!"

"It's lovely," Silver said of the black opal. Then, looking into her eyes, he repeated, "You're lovely."

She tucked her necklace back under her sweater. She hooked his arm tighter, bit her lower lip, and recanted, "Silver, give me a couple of days. I need to be alone."

He almost warned her that "alone" was no fun, and he would know. He had tried it for years. In his mind, he anticipated leading her up the steps of Hardwick College and carrying her like a bride into his room on the fifth floor. He saw himself unbuttoning the top button of her blouse with his nibbling teeth. He was hungry. No, he was more than hungry. He was thirsty for the sweat that would build up on her breasts after he posted himself between her legs and they got rocking.

"Silver, just wait until Sunday." She scrunched up the corner of her mouth. "Please, just two days. I'll see you here on Sunday." Her eyes gazed back at Starbucks. "Like today, at nine."

Silver scrunched up the corner of his own mouth, already imitating her gestures. Would his be the only lips he would taste today?

"But Linda," he whined.

She pressed a finger to his mouth. She smoothed the arm of his coat, but the wrinkles remained. And Silver's forehead remained wrinkled with worry when she took a step away from him and repeated, "This Sunday, at nine. Just like now." She pulled back the sloppy collar of his shirt and kissed him on the neck, a kiss whose suction lifted the skin. As she twirled around, her coat flared momentarily and then fell back against her body that—good God—he had once known and might know again.

Exile from the human touch of a good woman.

After she was gone, Silver returned to Starbucks and,

hands cupped, peered through the plate glass window at the table where they had sat like lovers. If only he had gotten the words right . . . He admonished himself for this failure. Another party had claimed the table, a man and a woman. Neither of them was smiling as they picked at Danish rolls, the tips of their sticky fingers going into their mouths. He drew away from the window, sighed at what had come and gone, and nearly jumped. At the curb stood his mother, scrutinizing the debris in the gutter as if searching for his watery remains. She spat in the gutter and stirred it with the stick in her hand. The sight saddened him.

"Mom? Is that you?" he called meekly.

When she raised her attention from the gutter, it seemed to him she was sucking on a sewing needle. On closer inspection he saw it was a long whisker on her chin that shone in the morning light. She tossed the stick aside.

"Where have you been?" she asked. Tears began to surge from her eyes.

"Not there!" he snapped, pointing to the gutter. A Milky Way wrapper floated past. He caught sight of his mother's tears, two streams of an incomprehensible sadness. He was suspicious.

"I've been looking for you," she sobbed.

"Well, I ain't been there!" His repeated anger sounded hollow, the voice of a boy hollering through a toilet roll.

Although he judged the tears on her cheeks were real, he was cautious. He wasn't about to forgive her just because she was sad about his departure. Hell, she could be crying over the three bananas he swiped from her fruit bowl.

Silver had planned a silent retreat to a bench where he could shuffle in his mind the details of his encounter with Linda. He desired such a respite so he could pet the arm of the coat to which she had clung tenderly. What better sweet sorrow than to open and close the collar and relive the kiss she had placed on his neck? It was something to do in private, a self-inspection in which he would lace his fingers together and let his heart buckle from lost love. Now he was staring at his mother, the whisker on her chin quivering. She was crying, although in the distance a passerby might take her emotional outburst to be laughter. She was ruining everything.

"Your grandfather died!" she sobbed.

Silver's heart dropped. He touched his stomach as if attempting to lift his heart back into its rightful place.

"That's why I'm looking for you, smarty-pants!" Her stern face steamed like an iron. Her tears freckled her cheeks but would soon disappear if her anger flared up.

"Ah, Mom," he consoled. He let down his guard and went to her. "Grandpa's dead?"

"No, don't." She blocked his hug with a stiff arm.

She had never gotten along with her father, a former

silver miner from Arizona, who himself was hard as flint. Every Christmas when young Silver unwrapped his presents—a box of pencils, coloring books, a cheap watch with no battery (he had to go buy it with his own money)— she recounted to Silver how her father spent nothing on them, even going so far as to tear up the upholstery from old couches to make their clothes. The front of one jumper was the cushion where people sat and previously rubbed their bottoms. She used these stories to temper Silver's disappointment over cheap gifts.

"I can't believe Grandpa Basilio's dead." Although he had only met him six or seven times, Silver presumed he was one of those old men who would sit in the sunlight on the front porch forever and ever.

"I need you to carry the casket." She made this more of an order than a request, then grumbled that she had lost two days of work because she had to spend her time tracking him down. She pinched her nose when she said that she searched at the Rescue Mission and the St. Vincent de Paul shelter and even the bus station at midnight. Embarrassed, she had scanned three parks to see if he was curled up on a bench, asleep. She wiped away a tear, her index finger working downward like a squeegee on her cheek.

"Am I the only pallbearer?" he asked, ignoring her litany of places where, indeed, he had occasionally sought refuge. He saw himself with the casket in his arms while he labored to climb the steps of a church, bells tolling from high above in pigeon-infested rafters. It was always hard labor burying relatives. Now he not only had to pray and reflect on the dead but also to carry the casket. He pictured an ant with a log in its teeth. He felt exhausted.

"No, he has one friend to help." She blew her nose into a cumulus-shaped cloud of Kleenex. "But can you get some of your friends to help? The funeral is tomorrow at ten, *mi'jo*." She furnished her face with remorse by batting her eyelashes and pouting her already turned down mouth.

"My friends?" he asked meekly. His two close friends, both poets, were full of complaint at the least effort. They even abhorred the simple exercise of lifting a pencil and writing a poem, no matter how thin the subject. How would they ever lift a casket of someone they didn't know? Also, if he remembered correctly, he owed both of them money. But there was Felipe, who he presumed was seated in front of his computer, eyes lit with a spreadsheet of stocks going up, not down. Could he take time off? he wondered. As a last resort, he could call the Chabran brothers, who Silver bet at that hour in the morning were wrestling for space in a dirty bed.

"He's your grandfather," she snapped, suddenly through with the kind mother act. "Can't you do this for me? Can't you find some of your smart friends? Can't you help your own mother?" Each fiery eye reddened with the full bloom of a struck match. Then, like a match, the flames quieted and finally died. But the smoke swirled in her pupils. "That Linda girl don't call no more."

"She's a woman, not a girl," Silver corrected.

"How do I know who she is!" Her hands rose to her hips, padded with fat.

Silver was too weak to reprimand his mother for bringing up the name of a woman who, less than ten minutes ago, was on his arm. Her clean smell was still pressed to his throat. "When did Grandpa die?"

"They don't know. They just found his body in his house."

His grandfather was from Mexico and had crossed the border at Nogales when he was fifteen, wet behind the ears and still wearing huaraches. That was all Silver knew; his grandfather's name never came up.

"How did it happen?"

"How do I know?" his mother asked angrily. "Am I God? Do I know how people die? The heart just stops!"

Silver rocked on the heels of his shoes. He had asked what he assumed was a proper question, and a snake hissed from her mouth.

His mother softened. "Remember when he bought you a bike?"

Silver remembered, all right. The bike was used, and both front and back tires were flat.

"And he took you to the river?"

Silver remembered that time as well. He had to pitch in a dollar for gas.

"And he took you to the fair?"

He recalled the fair bitterly. His grandfather just showed him the cows and pigs, not the rides, and prodded him to the drinking fountain when Silver asked for a soda.

"Wasn't that nice of Grandpa?" The smoke in her eyes began to kick up flames.

"Okay, okay," Silver whined, his mother having gained entry to his Catholic guilt.

"There's something else I want to say." She brought the Kleenex to her mouth and appeared to gag on her words. "But I can't, mi'jo. God will punish me in time."

What did she mean by that? Silver wondered. He evaluated his mother's sorrow, an emotion as foreign to her as Spain. It didn't make sense. Was she grief stricken or just plain crazy?

Head down, he towered over his mother as they walked to her car, parked on Jefferson Street. From there, he could see the lake where the two geese barely glided on the water, their webbed feet no doubt touching bottom and unsettling the claylike muck with each step.

"The service is at Samuel's Mortuary," she informed

Silver. She unlocked the door of her Dodge Colt, whose cabin gave off the scent of soap his mother scavenged in cereal boxes from her job at the laundry.

"Oh, Jesus," Silver moaned, although he did try to suppress this call for help because he feared that Jesus might actually show up and not walk steadily on the lake but come tripping over the potholes that lay at the bottom.

"Don't take the Lord's name," his mother scolded.

Silver suppressed a second moan. He had just been there for Al's service, and now he would have to return? Life did repeat itself, he confessed, and with each repetition he received the same spoonful of shitty luck.

"It's on High Street."

Silver assured his mother he knew the place.

"Be there by nine with your friends." She got into the car, started the motor gently, and rolled down the window. Out flew her hand, which gripped a white paper bag. "Here's some lunch."

He accepted the bag from his mother. Only when she drove away did he peer inside to discover half of a deli sandwich, which reminded him of his Native American brother and his daily excursion into the store for his daily handout. He could cry for every man and woman who must roam for food. Was this his mother? Was this a handout that the poor would discover in a garbage can?

Silver made out the quacking of geese on the lake. He migrated over to the lake and leaned over the short chain-link fence. The long-necked geese paddled toward him when he broke off a piece of the sandwich. He considered flinging the whole thing at the geese, not out of meanness but in the hurry to get these fowl grubbing on true nourishment. But he realized that to fling food at another was the kind of rude gesture the rich employed on the poor. Instead he held out the torn pieces in his extended hand, the bills of the geese clacking like the sound of plastic bodies of Ken and Barbie.

"Eat, little brothers," Silver demanded, motherly. "I wish I had more to give you." He was envisioning a wild-life refuge where no one would bother them when suddenly, a drop plopped on the surface of the water. Was this the start of another rain shower? When a second drop followed, he held out his palm. He gazed up and back down. He determined that the drops hadn't come from the sky but from his face. He wiped his eyes and blew his nose on the paper bag. A third and fourth drop fell, the pressure of his tears hardly making a dent on the surface. Then he heard a call, "Brother! Long time! Lost my coat you got me, but I bring you something tasty!" When he turned away from the geese, whose bills were still clacking for free eats, Silver saw that it was Armstrong, his street brother, wagging a large white bag at him. His smile was wide, too wide for anyone's good. Silver winced at Armstrong's ruined teeth. And yes, his trench coat was gone.

"Chinese people nicer than you or me think," Armstrong yelled as he approached. "And they cook better than you Mexicans!" His laughter scared away the geese but attracted two scrawny pigeons from the telephone wire. The two birds pecked at the muddy dents of Silver's shoe prints that began to slowly fill with water as he and Armstrong walked away together.

Silver, Armstrong, and Felipe all arrived at ten to nine at Samuel's Mortuary, dressed in dark suits pilfered from the abandoned inventory of the clothing store at Hardwick College. The night before, Felipe paced their small cubicle and argued that he couldn't possibly help, admitting he was scared of funeral homes. He recounted to Silver how he had lived next to one for three months when he was a child. Whenever a body was embalmed, a fan would go on and, to Felipe's nine-year-old imagination, the spirit of the dead person would float over the roof and settle on the lawn where he played marbles, a lone game of jacks, or kick the can. He was spooked when the wind scattered a pile of leaves, believing that it was a dead child at play.

But Armstrong enjoyed the opportunity to dress up for an occasion, even if it was to bear the weight of a man whose name he couldn't pronounce. He had located mismatched cuff links and a pair of shoes. Granted, one shoe was a size ten and the other a ten and a half, and his feet were a flat-footed size nine. But they were shoes that only needed a light dusting to make them glow.

"Shit, his grandpa is dead!" Armstrong scolded Felipe when he suggested that he wait in the car. "I never knew the man. Can't even say his name right." He looked at Silver. "Basalamo?"

"Basilio," Silver corrected.

"That's the man!" To Felipe, who was nervously combing the hair on the back of his hand, Armstrong preached, "Let's do him right."

The three stood in front of the closed mortuary.

Felipe turned his complaint from the burying of the dead to his tight-fitting suit. The armholes of the jacket dug into his flesh, and the pant cuffs ended around his ankles, exposing his legs to blasts of cold air. His throat was choked by a tie fashionable during Dwight D. Eisenhower's first term. He pulled at his collar, seeking a gasp or two of fresh air.

Armstrong attempted to peek into the stained glass

window. He pushed back the mail slot and let his eye rove wildly. "Even if we early, he's got to be in there. No way he can get up and hurry away. You know what I mean?"

Silver knew what he meant. How could his grandfather, dead more than three days—the Christian cutoff for rising up and proclaiming one thing or another—push back the lid of his coffin and, one leg first, then the other, jump from his cushioned resting place? Since he was a stiff old man, his juices were nearly dried at the end of his life and, subsequently in death, they would have been ossified. With or without a casket, the dead were difficult to move.

"How you know each other? I'm curious," Armstrong asked Silver and Felipe. "Your friend here has a business and, amigo, you from the street. How come you together?"

Silver eyed Felipe, and Felipe did the same in return. They had known each for so long that they had forgotten how their friendship, such as it was that morning, had begun.

"From protests," Silver answered.

"What kind of protests?"

"Protests against the establishment," answered Silver.

A bewildered Armstrong cocked his head left, then right. "Boy, that don't work. You got to steal if you wanna change things. People pay attention when things get gone."

Armstrong was explaining his theory of good theft and

bad theft when a large Buick pulled into the driveway. The driver gunned the engine, then cut it. Momentarily, out stepped the man they would soon learn was the assistant mortuary director, a heavyset black man named Moses Thatchgill. His suspenders held back a large belly that quivered with each step. His tie was the color of dark blood in a syringe. He approached the three of them with his arms at his sides. On any other man, they would be swinging. But on this man, they were dead at his sides. If he had pistols, he would have whipped them out and shot the three loiterers in front of his property, thus picking up more business for some other mortuary that dealt with riffraff.

"Where you been?" Armstrong asked, none too courteously.

"I been at home," the assistant funeral director answered.

"And when you was at home, we been here waiting."

"For what?" the man boomed.

Armstrong placed his arm on Silver's shoulders. "For to bury his grandfather Basalamo. What's wrong with you? And what's your name?"

"Ain't nobody to bury this morning. And my name is Moses Thatchgill, the assistant director of this establishment. Member of the white, Hispanic, and black chambers of commerce."

"Damn, brother, you connected!" Armstrong cried with laughter. "Got all the angles in your corner."

Mr. Thatchgill ignored Armstrong.

Silver took a business card from Mr. Thatchgill, who reiterated that there was no one to bury.

"What you mean here, Moses?" Armstrong shouted, his arms flinging skyward. "Don't you read the newspaper? Shit, there's got to be a black or brown soul to bury every second of the day!"

Felipe stepped away, ash colored, and feigned a commanding interest in the paper cup at the far end of porchlike entry of the funeral home.

Silver spoke up. He asked whether there was a Mexican person—dead, of course—in his care. The director shook his head. The body had been moved to Rodriguez Mortuary on Foothill Avenue, catty-corner to Perla's Tamale Heaven. He said the family couldn't pay for the expense of *their* burial.

"You mean if you ain't got the money, you don't get buried?" Armstrong asked hotly. He invited an answer. "Moses, my friend, part the waters on my question."

The man simply nodded. He was the kind of man who was not going to part the waters unless he was getting paid. And with dead people, family always paid.

"Shit!" an outraged Armstrong hollered. "I guess in my case I'm going to stay around for a long time! Who's going to bury my ass?" His laughter could have shooed a tree full of blackbirds into the next county.

"I'd bury you," Silver answered. He turned to Felipe, who was still studying the paper cup. "Huh, Felipe."

Felipe nodded in agreement.

"You're a good friend, Silver." Armstrong extended his arm for a handshake of their own peace accord.

"I do have papers on our costs if you're interested."

"Fuck those papers. I ain't ready to go, except to a smoky bar."

Moses Thatchgill put his hand to his chin. His rimless glasses winked in the faint sunlight that illuminated the clouds that would otherwise be dark and ominous. He shook a large finger at Armstrong. "Seems like I buried someone like you before."

"Shit!" Armstrong hollered to holy heaven. "And I come back!" Bent over in laughter, he slapped his thighs. He straightened up. "It take a lot to kill poor people like me. They starve you, brother Moses, and put you in wars and prisons and shit. What we niggers"—he gestured to Silver—"and Mexicans do is get strong. You hear a better truth than what I'm saying, mister?"

Mr. Thatchgill's mighty groan stretched his suspenders. He pulled up his sagging pants.

Armstrong smoothed both sleeves of his jacket, which ended above his wrists. "Where do you think we got this jacket, Moses?" He didn't wait for an answer because he was building up to a commercial enterprise. He told the man that in his business of burying folks he must be looking for jackets and pants. "Me and my friends can get you all sorts of clothes for burying."

"Clothes come from the family."

"That might be right," Armstrong countered, a wet smile brightening his outlook. "But just say that a family forgot a tie or a shirt or the body don't be wearing the right one once they seen them in the casket. You know, the shirt clashes with the color of the casket."

Silver envisioned one of those wide-lapel shirts fashionable in the seventies on a dead body.

"Say they missing the pants!" Armstrong yelled, although Mr. Thatchgill was only two feet away, not across the street where, at that hour of the morning, two kids were riding their bikes through the lake that had formed from a stopped-up drain hole. "You can't go like that all your dead life."

Silver sensed that the assistant funeral director wanted this talk in front of his establishment to end. On the back of his business card, he scribbled the address of the Rodriguez Mortuary. He handed it to Felipe, the sane one, he presumed.

Armstrong fumed. He wasn't done. "So if you see me on the street dead, you don't pick me up." When Moses didn't answer, Armstrong scolded, "Is that how it is?"

"Armstrong," Silver said, trying to pull his friend away.

"Nah, man!" Armstrong swore. "I just axed a question about this man's morals. I buried dogs I didn't know. I seen a momma cat run over in front of my auntie's house, and what you think I do? I go get the shovel. I dug holes for rats that came into my house to eat. Whacked them first, then buried the little suckers in decent graves." His voice rose in pitch. "Mr. Moses, you got a biblical name, but you ain't that. You partial to cheese, motherfucker? You a rat, motherfucker?"

Mr. Thatchgill's face paled. He took a step backward, sucking in his big belly, tightening up what muscle lay under the fat as he prepared himself for a punch to his almighty gut.

Silver and Felipe pulled Armstrong away. Mr. Thatchgill was busily licking his lips as he fumbled the key into the door. He had seen enough dead people not to want to be one.

They hustled Armstrong to the car.

"Man, you shouldn't have talked to him like that," Silver said after Armstrong calmed down.

Armstrong reflected. "Yeah, I should have thrown a casket on his big ole head."

"Violence never solves anything," Felipe said.

"Words ain't violence. It's when you bring out your pistol and blood flows. That's violence." Armstrong sucked on the inside of his cheek. "Dang, I'm wrong about that. Violence is when one dude shoots and the other shoots back. It don't come from one—how do you Mexicans say 'guy'?"

"*Vato,*" Silver said.

"Yeah, it comes from two *vatos*. One motherfucker firing and the other firing back. It's the philosophy of it takes two to tangle and only one to walk away."

The three of them drove a mile to the Rodriguez Mortuary. This business appeared closed—disease, shootings, and suicides having taken a day off. Only Silver's mother's Dodge Colt sat in the parking lot. The lights of the funeral home were out, though Silver picked up the sound of canned organ music.

"This one looks closed, too," Felipe said with a chuckle. "Let's go have breakfast, on me."

Silver's mother appeared from the mortuary, one foot holding the heavy door open. "Where have you been? I said nine."

Silver groaned when he saw his mother, his shoulders sagging like the beams in an old house. He didn't bother to inquire why she had moved his grandfather from one mortuary to another, although he suspected it had something to do with the imitation leather purse that hung on her arm—cheapness. He introduced his friends, and they all shook her hand and offered their condolences.

"I'm glad that my son has friends," said his mother. She pulled up close to Silver and began to straighten his tie, loosening it first and then drawing it up so it pinched like a noose. All he needed was a tree to swing from.

Silver noticed that the hair on her chin was gone. He also noticed that his mother's face was overly powdered and, in a spark of insight, he envisioned her as the one who was dead, not his grandfather. He saw a poem there, about rubbery cheeks flushed with red where no human blood flowed under the surface of skin.

She fixed the ties on both Felipe and Armstrong, who let out a gagging noise. As quickly as she turned her back on the two, they quickly loosened their ties and breathed deeply, something the dead in the mortuary couldn't enjoy.

They entered the mortuary and solemnly shuffled into a small chapel where a young man in a khaki-colored gardening outfit was taking away a wreath of flowers still emitting a sweet smell. The three of them were heading to seat themselves in the middle pew, a respectful distance from the casket in the front. But Silver's mother shouted, "No, we don't have time for that. We're late as it is." She beckoned them to follow her but abruptly signaled for them to wait. She disappeared from the small chapel.

In the front pew sat a small elderly man with his age-peppered hands cupped around his ears. When this man spun around, Silver confronted Rudy Padilla, the printer. Rudy winced at Silver. Recognizing him, he shouted, "You skinny so-and-so!"

"Good God!" Silver yelled, then clapped his hand over his mouth. His outburst showed disrespect.

Rudy approached Silver. "I'm sorry about your father."

"No, grandfather," Silver corrected.

Rudy peered over Silver's shoulder at his mother, who had a Kleenex up to her mouth. He stalled, as if he were trying to remember something.

"You so-and-so." Rudy laughed. "I known your grandpa when he came over. He was a strong worker in the mines. Never got hurt, except when he hit himself in the head with a pickax." He stuck out a hand, gray as newsprint. Silver, not knowing what to do, put out his hand. Rudy next extended a hand to Armstrong. "I'm Rudy Padilla. Used to be a printer until I couldn't stand no more." He shook hands with Felipe, who kept fitting his eyeglasses back on his oily nose. The oils of nervousness had moistened his face.

Armstrong looked from Silver to Rudy and back to Silver. "Amigo, you know people in the strangest places."

This allegation struck Silver as a savvy truth. Just five

days ago, he was at Al's funeral and now he was at another one, this one where there were more corpses than
mourners—he had spied five caskets waiting in the wings
of the hallway. At this rate, he should get himself a decent suit for upcoming funerals.

Rudy pointed to his ear when he had called Armstrong
"Randy" and Armstrong had shouted that he would bear
no white boy's name. "I can't hear good."

"How's your smelling?" Armstrong asked.

"What?"

"Your smelling is bad, too, 'cause you got too much
cologne on, brother." Armstrong waved his hand in front
of his face.

With his fingers like pliers, Rudy brought out the small
hearing aids from the nests of hairy ears. "Government
paid for these. Over in the Korean War a bomb exploded
on a buddy of mine. I was eight feet away. Hurt my ears
and killed him pretty good."

"Jesus," Silver moaned.

Felipe shaded his eyes, as if shrapnel was still flying.
He was upset at the course of the conversation and asked,
"Can't we talk about something else?"

"What?" Rudy called.

Silver shook his head and shouted, "Nothing!"

Silver's mother had left the chapel and returned with
the funeral director, who said in Spanish that he was sorry

for the family's loss. He pursed his lips at Armstrong, confused by his presence.

The funeral director took the lead by reciting a brief
prayer for the deceased in Spanish. "Amen," he mumbled.

Armstrong pulled on Felipe's sleeve. "Amen is same
in Spanish like it is in English?"

Felipe nodded.

Armstrong muttered under his breath, "Damn, you
learn something every minute if you only listen." He
looked at Rudy, who was fiddling with one of the hearing
aids. "Ah, yeah, except for some folks."

Silver's mother called Rudy over and spoke in a con-
spiratorial whisper. They gazed at Silver, who knew they
were talking about him. But he dismissed their conspira-
torial designs because after the funeral he had every intention of going his own way, and fast.

The four of them carried the casket to the hearse idling
in the driveway. None of them was breathing hard, the
load of wood and flesh being surprisingly light.

"I'm going to take my own car," Silver's mother said.

Silver knew why. After the service, she was going to
go to work, which wasn't more than a mile from the cemetery. This much she despised her father. Otherwise why
did her Kleenex go to her sweaty brow instead of to a pair
of crying eyes?

The white-gloved driver closed the back door. He

hurried around to open the door for the four of them.

"Silver, I just can't go," Felipe begged nervously. It was as if he were in the coffin and he was reluctant to depart. "You take my car and drive it back. I'll hop on a bus."

Silver thanked Felipe. He understood Felipe's childhood trauma of living next to a funeral home. He also understood that the suit was tight fitting. Felipe's throat was red from the constant tugging at his collar.

Since they were a small party of three mourners, they were allowed to ride in the hearse at no extra charge. Rudy sat next to the driver, a silent figure with the legs of a praying mantis, and Silver and Armstrong hunkered down in the back.

"This is nice," Armstrong muttered, venting his appreciation of fine living as he pinched the leather seat. He adjusted the air-conditioning on his left shoe, the bigger of the two. "Hardly walked and my feet are hurting me from these shoes being loose!" His laughter prompted Rudy to scream, "What?"

The hearse pulled onto the road and accelerated, thrusting leaves out of their path.

"The ride is smooth, too," Armstrong commented.

"What are you saying?" Rudy screamed. "It's not polite to talk behind a person's back."

Armstrong screamed to Rudy, "Let me see one of 'em."

He poked a finger at his own ear.

Rudy picked at the left hearing aid until it came out and handed it to Armstrong, who examined it closely and then fitted the device into his own ear. His eyes moved in their sockets as he appraised its use. When Rudy started to say something, Armstrong shushed him. He clicked his fingers for Rudy's other hearing aid. This, too, he fitted in his ear, and as they rode to the cemetery Armstrong picked up sounds that he had never heard before.

"These are like microscopes," he told Silver, "but for the ears. You know what I mean?"

"What!" Rudy screamed. He was like a child on his knees, eager to join the backseat conversation.

Armstrong plucked the devices from his ears. "You need these more than anybody I know." He cast a glance over his shoulders at the casket adorned with a single flower, its perfume overwhelmed by the scent lassoed around Rudy's neck. "Well, with all due respect, almost everybody."

Silver was surprised that his mother cried like a child. After the four of them sprinkled dirt onto the casket, she tearfully offered him the key to his grandfather's house. "Take anything you want from the house, *mi'jo.*" She pressed an ancient skeleton key into his palm. She told him that her father would want him to have some of his personal things. She gave him the address on the back of an old envelope.

Silver spanked his palm with the key. To him, it seemed like a joke—what skeletons would he find at his grandfather's house?

"I had one like that," Rudy remarked. "Stabbed a man with it when he said he wouldn't pay his printing bill." He chuckled with his hands cupped around his ears, ready to catch the hearing aids if they popped out from his excitement. "Well, I didn't really stab him. More like poked. But pokes hurt too if you get it in the throat."

Armstrong peeled open his shirt and revealed the silky scar of a knife wound. "Touch it," Armstrong commanded Rudy. "It's like silk. I done got cut when I was nineteen."

Rudy ran a finger down Armstrong's belly, dented with a scrub board of ribs. He proceeded to roll up his pants leg. His own scar snaked up his leg, and where it ended, Silver didn't wish to ask. "Got this from the shrapnel when my buddy got killed."

Armstrong touched Rudy's scar and whistled. "How did it feel when you got hit?"

"Like a bee sting," he answered directly. He had answered the question before.

Armstrong smiled in agreement. "That's how it is,

brother." He shook hands with Rudy and remarked that they had more in common than what meets the common eye in a common head.

"We're almost alike, huh?" Rudy appreciated the man-to-man discourse on body wounds.

"Yeah, except you can't hear, and I can."

Rudy caroled his laughter over the deaf tombstones and instructed Armstrong to touch the knot he received when his first wife banged him with a glass ashtray while he was sleeping off a New Year's hangover.

"Been there too," Armstrong crowed wisely. "Girl-friend of mine hit me with a TV tray all 'cause I said her wig was too big."

By then his mother had left his side, hurrying over the rain-muddied grass to her car. Silver himself had stepped away from the two as they counted their wounds and were now moving on to the lost inventory of teeth knocked out in fights. When each had his mouth open, like baby sparrows, Silver distanced himself farther from the two and scanned the headstones that rose up the hill and over the hill into a gully where the rain collected and seasonally washed over the dead.

Silver buried his grandfather without a rush of emo-tion, although he had been moved by his mother's sor-row. At the sight of the casket descending slowly into its dark hole, her face bunched up from heartfelt crying that jerked her shoulders. Other than anger, he had never seen such emotion come alive on her face. And he marveled at Rudy, who seemed not in the least bothered that he was in a cemetery he would certainly join in a matter of years.

Silver closed his eyes, his fingers massaging the bridge of his nose. When he opened them, Armstrong was poking him with a finger.

"You got any knife wounds on you?"

"Nah, just a bleeding heart," Silver caught himself saying. Over Armstrong's shoulders, he watched his mother's Dodge Colt pull out of the cemetery's parking lot. He swore he heard her tires squeal. This was how much she wanted to get away?

On their return to the mortuary, Silver was amazed that the parking lot was filled. Another burial was on its way. Even with the rolled-up windows, he could make out the sound of canned organ music. He imagined the heavy odor of lilies.

Armstrong and Rudy bid their farewells. If they had lived close to each other, in a duplex or a government project, they would be the kind of men who would sit under trees, playing checkers. Neither would cheat nor care if he won or lost. They would not be above sharing peach brandy, smacking their lips and babbling, "Mighty tasty stuff for the tummy. Not to mention a breath freshener if you gotta smack kisses on some women." But Rudy was installed in a rest home with blathering televisions drowning out the blather of the senile with uncombed hair and lipstick applied all the way to their chins. Armstrong had yet to find a door to enter and close. He was homeless. Neither was going to pull a woman into his arms and start kissing her anytime soon.

"Now, I didn't say yet how sorry I was about your grandpa." Armstrong offered his condolences. He then winced at the sound of the Volvo's muffler clanging against the chassis as the car picked up speed. "What the fuck's wrong down below?"

Down below? Silver drew a portrait of hell in the start of the week. But this hell disappeared when he gazed in the rearview mirror—a white shark of a police cruiser was behind them. Two short-haired officers with thick necks sat up front. The cruiser passed, its windows glinting like knives. Silver noticed that the back was empty and the officers were merrily off in search of some lazy soul to cage inside. One of the officers eyed Silver nastily.

Silver made certain that both his hands were on the steering wheel. It had been a while since he had driven a car, and perhaps there were new laws. He also realized that his license was expired. Like on his old passport, he wouldn't resemble the face on his driver's license.

Armstrong was oblivious to the police. "And I know we just met on the street, but I was glad that you asked

me to help out." He undid his tie like a businessman at
the end of the day. "Nearly passed out the way your mother
fixed my tie."

Silver was warmed by Armstrong's sincerity, touched
that this person he hardly knew had volunteered to carry
his grandfather's casket. "I'm glad, too. You're all right,
brother."

Silver drove over to Casper's on Broadway, where they
ordered hot dogs, a large bag of barbecue potato chips, and
orange sodas. Armstrong pulled at the napkin dispenser
until it was empty. The manager watched Armstrong's
activity, but since he was busily slapping mustard on an
office order of eighteen hot dogs, plus whacking back
flames rising off the oily griddle, he just made a face and
snarled over the sizzling meat.

Armstrong praised his order. "I like dogs that stick
out on both ends." He held up one of his hot dogs: The
meaty ends stuck out obscenely from the bun.

They ate in silence, although a fly visited their table
and buzzed over their heads. Silver fathomed his poetic
mind: Damn fly's making a halo over our heads. And flies,
in any season, meant death. He calculated its spins over
Armstrong's head and the spins over his own head: Unless his arithmetic was wrong, the fly made nineteen trips
over his skull to nine over Armstrong's. Was this a prophecy? Was death locating a place to settle and rub its greasy

hands together? The hot dog in his throat became clogged, and only a long swallow of orange soda dislodged it from his windpipe.

"What's wrong?" Armstrong asked. "Dog go down the wrong alley?" he asked, touching his throat.

Although a wordsmith, Silver couldn't locate the words to critique the terror he foresaw in the fly. So he mentioned Linda. He enlightened Armstrong on their pasts—the good parts only, not his shameless act of bedding her down a few delightful times and letting her go—and how had he recently rekindled his love for her.

"I done that, too," Armstrong said. "The second time around with a woman is better 'cause you get right down to business." He smirked like a duck, then giggled with a napkin hiding his face.

"You want to hang with me?" Silver asked Armstrong, who had his fist inside the potato chip bag, dabbing up with his licked fingers the last flakes. "I'm going to my grandfather's place."

"Let me look at my calendar." He brought out a small notebook and flipped through its pages, all the while sopping up mustard with a wad of napkins from the corners of his mouth. He announced, "I is free to go as I please." He giggled at his half rhyme of *free* and *please,* two words he employed alternatively on a daily basis.

They drove to Silver's grandfather's house in San

Leandro, stopping three times at gas stations and convenience stores for directions. Each time Armstrong climbed
out of the car to look underneath at the muffler. The rattling was making him edgy.

"Sounds like prisoners beating spoons on the bars,"
Armstrong complained.

Finally Silver located the house, parked the car in the
driveway, and procured from his pocket the skeleton key
that had been poking his thigh. He was nervous. His imagination became inflated. What if when he opened the front
door, his grandfather's spirit came limping out and, by
chance, Silver breathed in a little of the spirit's exhaust as
it passed? What then? Would he become like his grandfather, a stingy soul?

Silver counted on finding some object worth selling,
something that he could pitch right in front of Hardwick
College. Then again, he could use a second coffeepot and
set of nearly new towels. He could also use a mattress,
but on second thought he didn't savor the prospect of sleeping where his grandfather might have died. He had never
asked his mother when and where the neighbors had found
his body. Perhaps his grandfather succumbed at his kitchen
table, next to a twice-dipped tea bag sitting in a soup spoon.

But no gush of grandfatherly spirit whistled from the
front door when he nudged it open with his body. A neighbor from across the street appeared from behind the screen

door. Silver waved a friendly hello, but the person quickly disappeared, the screen door slapping shut behind him.

"Come on in when you're done," Silver yelled to Armstrong, who had crawled under the Volvo to investigate the rattling.

Silver stepped cautiously into the house. The floor creaked as he advanced to the center of the living room. He considered calling out, "Hello," but who would answer? His fingers ran down a dusty lamp and tested the springs of the spongy couch. He picked up a candy dish from the coffee table and placed it back down. The television was a cabinet-style set made of wood and plastic from the 1960s and would be too heavy and awkward to lift— the front door was narrow and the floor warped and rotted from the mighty appetite of termites and other critters. He, Armstrong, and the television risked plunging through the floor.

In the kitchen, the faucet dripped into a bowl that, to Silver's way of thinking, might have held his grandfather's last supper. He noticed the curtains that were freakily torn, as if a madwoman had raked them with her long fingernails. But the curtains were just old and moth-eaten and perhaps peeled back so repeatedly to spy on the neighbors that they just became shreds. He yanked open the refrigerator. With the bulb out, Silver had no penchant to feel around for a soda. He had screamed through too many horror movies to think that a lobsterlike hand would never dwell in the crisper.

He hurriedly abandoned the kitchen and wandered into the bedroom that held a bed, two lamps, extension cords that worked the lamps from one socket, and photographs on the walls. He approached the photographs, most of them in frames but some taped on the wall and curled from age. There were photos of family members in Mexico, all with twilight in their eyes. He set a theory going in his mind: Maybe that's where I get my poetry. Dark matter. The purplish shadow on a sandy hill. The cloudy waters where both man and beast drink.

"Good God!" Silver blurted out. His finger had located his mother and an older man in a photograph, possibly a wedding portrait because the couple were standing in front of a church. He unhooked the photograph from the wall and brought it to his face: Yes, on closer inspection, it was a wedding portrait. His mother was dressed in white and the man was in a striped suit, a gold pocket watch gleaming on the vest. The man appeared sturdy, a worker no doubt, with lines on his brow from squinting into the sun. His mother's face was already pulled down in a perpetual pout.

"Damn," he muttered as he placed the portrait back onto the wall. "Mom married an old cowboy."

There was also a photograph of the couple a few years

later. But in this, another man about his mother's age stood next to her, straw hat in hand. Who was this poor cow rustler? He was dressed in overalls, and his head was as large as a cow's. The man was dark and ugly from having been pastured out in the sun for God knows how long.

"Mom couldn't have been married," he said, disregarding the facts before him. He sat on the edge of his grandfather's squeaky bed as he studied the ancient photos that included not only family members but also postcards of Yosemite, Pismo Beach, and Kings Canyon National Park of yesteryear. His mother had always told him he was just born, that there never had been a man in her life. Of course, he never believed in a virgin birth, either in this century or any other century, and he didn't believe in virgins, period, having never met one. He was certain his mother had stepped out of her panties at least once. Now he stood before her wedding portrait and other small pictures, taped and curled. Was it possible the old turkey in the photograph was *his* father?

Carefully he peeled them off like a Band-Aid and unhooked the pictures in the dusty frames. He placed them in a box and hollered, "Armstrong, my man," as he hustled from the bedroom to the living room. Kicking open the door, he hollered again for his friend in a higher pitch. He carried the past in his arms, escorting these righteous pictures of family to the Volvo in the driveway, when he felt something drop on his shoulder. For a moment, he assumed the weight of the hand belonged to Armstrong. Not a chance. When he snatched a look over his shoulder, he saw the hand was white, not black, meaty, not bony, and ready to close into a fist, not brotherly: The hand was attached to a pumpkin-shaped police officer who had enjoyed not only platters of meat but barrels of beer: The man was large.

"We've had a complaint," the officer, a natural baritone, said deeply. His lunch was still on his breath and a bloody clot on his chin from a wicked shave or the leftover splatter from a recent bout of fisticuffs. "What do you have in the box?"

"Pictures," Silver answered. "What did I do? I ain't done nothing." He scanned the surroundings and didn't come across Armstrong. Had his sidekick abandoned him in a dire moment?

"Are they dirty pictures?" the officer asked as he guided Silver roughly to the front lawn. The officer tried to grab the box, but Silver wouldn't let go—his past had just shown itself, and he wasn't about to give it up. Hell, no! He would hold on to it for dear life. But seconds later he broke that promise to his kin when a second officer appeared from behind and wrapped his arms around Silver's neck and the back of his head. It was a familiar choke hold from demonstrations of the seventies and one that sent the tongue lolling about like a snake.

Silver dropped to his knees, genuflecting to a greater power. When the pressure of the choke hold clicked a bone in his neck, he released the box to the officer, who tossed it aside, the photos flying like a deck of playing cards.

"Look at what you did!" The wedding portrait of his mother and the stranger (her husband?) was looking up at him.

The officer ignored Silver and slowly pressed a knee into the small of Silver's back. He frisked Silver's pockets for a wallet. Finding none, he pressed Silver's face into the grass, flattening the Roman architecture of his nose, the one part of his body with which he had any chance of attracting a woman. Now his flared nostrils were filling with the aroma of rain-spongy grass.

"That hurt me, man!" Silver screamed when the officer released pressure from the choke hold and his nose came up for a breath of fresh air. "That's my grandpa's house."

"Where's your identification?" asked the officer who had smashed his nose.

"Where's yours? I don't have to show you shit, unless it's on the bottom of my shoes."

The answer to his question sent Silver back into the grass for another sniff.

"It's not nice to break and enter," the baritone officer

growled when he let gasping Silver up for air. "Or to talk to us like we're your trash friends."

"I'm telling you, man. This is Grandpa's crib!" He spit out flakes of grass from his mouth. On his belly, Silver glimpsed a movement under the Volvo—a dangling fan belt, a loose water hose, or the muffler that had troubled Armstrong so? He saw the whites of two blinking eyes and had time to evaluate a set of teeth too yellow and broken to belong to a cat. There was also an elbow and a single finger like the udder of a cow. In all, these clues added up to the body parts Armstrong couldn't hide.

"Jesus!" Silver muttered.

This outburst brought his face back into the grass and a pinch of handcuffs onto his wrists.

"The name of Jesus is reserved for moments of prayer," the choke-holding cop warned.

But Silver *was* in prayer. He prayed that these beef-eaters would allow him to sit up and brief them on his life story. He would skip his past and lead them to near the present. He would first explain he was a poet in love with a woman Linda, a lovely name in any race. Surely romance affected all people, even those on the public dole like the two officers who spontaneously decided to drag Silver around the lawn for the heck of it. If love didn't ply their hearts, he would then point out his mother in one of the photos and assure them that they shared facial traits, except for his presently bent nose. He sniffed the liquids in his nostrils. Was that the ooze of blood in his throat?

"Jesus!" Silver called, but the Lord didn't answer.

"No more use of the Lord's name," the officer instructed him. "If you went to church, you might not be here."

There was truth to this observation. But no way in hell was he going to agree with him now that his mouth was filled not only with grass and blood but also a serving of mud. When Silver's face was released, he waited for his vision to clear. His friend was indeed clinging to the car chassis. Armstrong's face was long and sad at witnessing his friend's face repeatedly dunked in the grass. Hugging for dear life the cool parts of the chassis, he dared not get involved.

Silver was yanked to his feet, pushed back down to the lawn, and dragged none too nicely to an unmarked car. He was shoved into the back.

"You hurt my nose," Silver complained.

"You're lucky it's Lent," the religious officer responded. "Otherwise I would have hurt you all over."

Indeed, Silver was glad that it was Lent season. He abhorred the possibility of his entire body feeling like his nose. As the car slowly pulled away from the curb, he risked a glance at the Volvo: Armstrong, detached from the chassis but still lying low, was blinking like a cat. His friend threw up a hand to wave adios.

Silver was seated in the cubicle, his nose crusted with rings of blood. He considered picking at the blood or wiping it away with his shirtsleeve, but he intended to demonstrate his brutalized condition when his briefcase-toting lawyer appeared, breathless from leaping into action. He would petition for a young lawyer, not an alcoholic has-been with a nose like a red bell pepper and an immense belly cascading over his belt. God, he thought, if only they would assign him a female lawyer! They were tougher than men.

He was nearly driven to throw his head against the wall, thus raising a mountainous welt that would jump-start his counsel to file the costliest lawsuit since the beginning of the world. But he, a poet, was searching for truth to the mayhem that occurred on the front lawn of his grandfather's house. Also, he didn't relish the taste of pain.

The officers arrested him on suspicion of breaking and entering. They lumped together the use of profanity in a public place (he cussed up a storm when his head bounced on the curb) and resisting arrest, which was true because he did let his body go limp as the officers dragged him to the car, the heels of his shoes scarring up the lawn. Now he behaved himself in the cubicle, which he was beginning to frequent more often than he cared to.

He thought of his grandfather, buried earlier in the day, and fumbled with an image of Linda, the woman he would do more than die for. He would live for her by constructing an elaborate temple of poems that would take a lifetime. He fumbled with her image because he remembered her both as a young woman and one who had hit middle age. He was confused and was going to lather his lawyer with the spittle of confusion. Perhaps they could bring a suit against the city on one poet's inability to think straight.

"Mom," he called out. No, Silver wasn't hankering for his mother to smother him in her nurturing arms but to ask, "Who is the man in your wedding photo?" Fatherless, Silver had grown up with his mother, who, he admitted, labored like a father as a laundry worker—so what was his beef? When she came home, her skin was permeated with the scent of industrial soap, a nice disguise because her true humanly scent was a fragrance closer to the sweat of onions sizzling in a frying pan. He never asked about his father, and his mother, likewise, didn't bring him up. His father wasn't there for Boy Scouts, backyard boxing lessons, and delicate matters regarding the pros and cons of masturbation. In spring, when Silver's elementary school held a Chip Off the Old Block pancake drive to buy library books, Silver moped in his bedroom. He had no father. By seventh grade, however, he began to feel better about his nearly orphaned status because most of his friends' fathers had flown the coop. And those who remained home were assholes relegated to La-Z-Boy recliners.

"Dad," Silver called absently.

The door creaked open. A large hand gripped the doorjamb before it disappeared. A voice in the hallway called for a mop to clean up the spillage of vomit.

Silver swallowed. Was this Daddy at the door? If so, he hoped that his father would allow him to throw his head onto his shoulders and wail, "*Papi*, where have you been?" However, when he swallowed a second time, he tasted a lozenge of fear. Lieutenant Waldman heaved forth into the cubicle, a cup of coffee in one hand and three glazed doughnuts hooked on his thumb. The doughnuts looked like they were pitched onto his thumb in some carnival game.

But Silver was keenly aware that the cameo appearance of Lieutenant Waldman, followed by Sergeant Chin, didn't suggest a ride on the Tilt-A-Whirl unless the lieutenant had plans to swing him by his heels for the fun of it. And no, his presence didn't suggest a father-to-son talk in which there was shoulder patting and giggles regarding Daddy's first encounter with the female breast. Matters appeared serious. Sergeant Chin closed the door behind him.

"You want one?" Lieutenant Waldman asked, thrusting out his hand, an action that made the doughnuts spin on his thumb.

Silver waved away this offer of carbohydrates. "Seen what they done to my nose?"

Lieutenant Waldman smiled his set of lug-nut teeth. He bit a hunk from his doughnut and sipped his coffee. He rolled the carpet of his tongue throughout his mouth. He took another bite and finished up a second doughnut in three chomps.

"I'll admit," the lieutenant began, "these doughnuts are free and it didn't cost me anything other than a little energy to reach for them in the box over at the main office." He raised the coffee cup. "And this didn't cost me anything either." He smiled at Silver and uttered a he he he that rocked his massive shoulders. "So when I offer something, even if it didn't cost me shit, I want people to accept my generosity. We're here to serve." He laughed a jolly laugh at this last comment and patted the shoulders of stern-faced Sergeant Chin, who stood with his hands laced in front of his groin. The sergeant was always prepared. The lieutenant swiveled his head and lasered a grilling anger at Silver. "Get what I mean, Mendoza?"

Silver didn't dare correct the lieutenant on his name, not with the fire issuing from his eyeballs. Instead he turned his attention to the last doughnut on the lieutenant's thumb as it once again was raised in the gesture of, "Please, take one." He obliged by tugging the doughnut from the lieutenant's hand, which was no easy task because his corpulent thumb nearly filled the doughnut hole. He licked his lips, muttered a thank-you, and nibbled the doughnut like a squirrel. He had to admit, that sugar-coated monster of pastry tasted good.

The lieutenant took a folder from Sergeant Chin and began his inquiry. "Let's see, we've already taken care of the business with the bra. So that's solved." He read through the lower territory of his bifocal eyeglasses. "Yesterday you were arrested for . . ."

A jittery Silver spoke up none too politely with a doughnut in his mouth. "That was my grandfather's house. He died, and my mom said that I could go and get anything I want." The sweetness of the doughnut laminated his tongue, but his anger was as sour as wonton soup. He started to reach in his pocket for the skeleton key to the house but stopped when he recalled that the police had confiscated it. Plus Sergeant Chin had removed his hands from the front of his groin and was bringing them toward Silver's face, already hurting and in need of a shellacking of Bactine. Hands up, he promised, "Okay, okay, I'll be cool."

The lieutenant grinned evilly. The grin was a grin of an alligator two seconds before it snaps. "You know, Mendoza, you got to learn not to interrupt."

Silver was learning quickly. He sucked in his lips. When he spat them out, only air issued forth.

"I'm telling you that neighbors reported that some-one—meaning you, sucker—had entered Mr. Gomez's house."

Silver was baffled. Mr. Gomez?

"True, Mr. Gomez died from whatever, but a relative was assigned to pick up his personal items." He gestured toward the door, which Silver noted was grimy around the handle. "He's twiddling his thumbs in the hallway."

Silver wavered between inquiring about this Gomez person or remaining quietly sitting on his hands. A relative? Who was this guy? He had heard of relatives in Mexico, but he had never seen or heard of any here in California.

"This person says that he is the only one warranted to gather your grandpa's things. If, indeed, this dead fellow is your grandpa." The lieutenant took off his eyeglasses and rose from his chair. He stretched his arms toward the ceiling. To the sergeant, he concluded, "Looks like breaking and entering to me. Stealing from the dead.

My, my, Mendoza, that's pretty low, just above running over an old lady in the crosswalk." He *tsked-tsked* Silver, then licked his finger like a lollipop for a sugary taste of sticky doughnut glaze.

"Can I say something?" Silver asked.

"Well, since the fellow you call Gramps can't speak up, let's hear your story."

Silver began with his dream of going to Spain, economy class, and discovering the connection between Chicano and Spanish literature. He told them about the conference in Madrid. Madrid, he professed, was famous for its leather, silver, and marvelous red wine, which he planned to learn about by drinking as much as he could afford. Madrid was also home of the Prado, the third-largest art museum in the world. When the lieutenant yawned, he next spoke of Al's death, which still spooked him for reasons he would not disclose. When he threw out Linda's name, however, the lieutenant stopped Silver.

"Is that the gal with the bra?" the lieutenant bellowed.

Silver recoiled from the lieutenant's breath. Behind the scent of doughnuts flowered a stew from the day before.

The room became silent. The raking of predictable jail time could be heard on a wristwatch.

"Why in the fuck are you going out with a dead man's wife right away?" He leaned forward, his hands propped on his knees. "You oughta check out a manners book from the library. Don't you believe in a grieving period?"

"It's a long and private story," Silver braved, his chest ballooning proudly until the air in his lungs gave out and his chest returned to its usual deflated state. This was dangerous. If his chair had had arms, he would have gripped them because Lieutenant Waldman was peeling back his lips to reveal his teeth. The alligator look! Silver had come to know the lieutenant well enough to recognize anger. So he relented. "It's a long story, but I'm willing to tell it."

"Your story is lame. I oughta smack the rest of your mug so your nose won't be so lonely. Make your ears bleed through your anus." He fumed and popped a knuckle. "Yeah, you squirrel, I would smack you except I just ate some doughnuts and I have to honor that memory of that tasty snack." The lieutenant burped. He got up with a groan and paced, head down. But Sergeant Chin, all business, had his eyes locked on Silver.

Silver was convinced that he should fill out any form on the table necessary to lodge a complaint of police brutality. He was going to accuse the lieutenant of this and that when the door opened and another officer prodded a man into the cubicle. The officer left.

"Please come in, Mr. Gomez," Sergeant Chin said.

The man stepped shyly into the cubicle. His eyes were

beady, especially in a head that was large as a cow's. The man held the box of photographs from Silver's grandfather's house.

"Is he supposed to see me?" the man asked nervously.

The lieutenant waved a hand at Silver. "Don't worry about this squirrel. Let me ask you. Is he a relative of your family?"

"No," the man responded.

"You've never seen this man before?"

The man shook his large cow head.

"I ain't seen this creepy asshole either," Silver volunteered angrily. "He ain't family of mine!"

Angry, Sergeant Chin's eyes boiled in their slim and tidy sockets. The veins on his hands rippled with a surge of blood. "Don't say another word." He stepped not toward Silver but away, distancing himself for a proper snap kick that would sink deeply into Silver's empty gut.

Lieutenant Waldman apologized to Mr. Gomez for Silver's outburst. Again he asked Mr. Gomez if he had ever set eyes on the suspect seated in the chair, and once again Mr. Gomez wagged his large cow head. The wag was the wag of an animal shaking off flies. The man left with his box of photographs.

The lieutenant pulled a chair in front of Silver. "Now, what did I say? No one knows you."

Any other time Silver would have assumed he was

referring to his poetry career. But at that moment, not so. He hazarded a request. "I want to make a call."

The lieutenant giggled. He fit a finger into his mouth and worked the paste of his doughnut from a molar.

"I want to call my mom."

The lieutenant pushed his giggle into a hardy laughter. He leaned his arm onto Sergeant Chin's broad kung fu shoulders. Sergeant Chin allowed the corners of his mouth to lift into a smile. Then the sergeant's smile flattened in order to issue an accented, "Fuck you."

Silver was held because Mr. Gomez, his grandfather's son, he presumed, his mother's half brother, he figured, was going to press charges of trespassing. Also, the police department had the right to hold him for twenty-four hours, and Lieutenant Waldman assured Silver that it wouldn't hurt to fatten up on a little jail food. He remarked that the Jell-O came in the colors of red, green, and white, the colors of the Mexican flag.

Silver was whisked to a cell smothered in shadows because its one overhead bulb was out. He was alone. Or, at least, he was the only human within the confines that would make a gorilla pace. As soon as he entered the cell, a flea and his comrade, the louse, jumped from the sagging cot and onto his neck. From there, they had free rein with their clipperlike jaws. At first, Silver scratched and searched his neck, belly, arms, and legs for the critters. He found himself caring more about their destruction than his release.

Silver scratched until he gave up, frustrated. "Eat me!" he called out to the flea and louse, plus a mouse that showed up to wiggle its long whiskers and disappear back into the wall. His call also excited someone in a nearby cell, who responded in a high voice, "Give me the key to your cell, and I will."

After that, Silver became silent as a monk. He found solace at the clean edge of his otherwise dirty cot, where he compared his personal sadness as similar to the sadness of the geese at the city-made lake. He had it worse, he contended. The geese could always fly away or live perpetually on dropped bagels and half-eaten hot dogs. His self-pity evaporated when he began to mull over why he was a Mendez and this other guy a Gomez. What kind of family do I come from? he wondered. He was recounting the photos, possibly snatched for good, when he heard the crank of a key in the main gate, the sigh of its pressurized release, and the thud of footsteps—one set was crisp and orderly and the other was the staggering shuffle of a drunk Frankenstein monster. The jailer opened up his cell and said snidely, "You have a visitor."

The visitor was a tall street brother with his wool beanie in his hands. He stank of drink and not very good drink—peach brandy in a bottle gripped by at least six other homeless brothers and passed around until only the backwash from their throats was left.

"It's raining out there," the visitor slurred. He brushed rain from the oily shoulders of his coat. Only a duck had more slick oils to fend off water.

Silver pictured his grandfather's grave in a lake of dark rainwater. The casket was rising from the ground and sailing off like a boat. Where it was headed, toward heaven or hell, Tulare or Fresno, he wasn't about to risk prophesying. He had hardly got to befriend his grandfather, though he recognized his stingy manner.

"Raining hard?" Silver asked in order to measure his cell mate's drunkenness.

The brother wiggled his pants cuffs. "Fuck, yeah! And it rained a brand-new bottle of brandy when the police grabbed it from my lips. Those crackers poured it right on my shoes." He stared down at his battered shoes. "It's like the Bible out there, you know, with that big ole boat where they got two of everything." He counted out elephants, chimpanzees, butterflies, snakes if they be nice, and winos!

Silver blinked at the brother.

"Yeah, it could be you and me." He staggered a bit

and sat safely on the cot. "You a wino, ain't you?"

Silver would assume such a title if it meant he could weigh anchor with the animals and get safely out of town. "Sometimes."

"Sometimes is sufficient to get on board. Just raise one sail and we get onto something better."

The brother lectured Silver about how after a rain comes fog and after the fog more rain followed by mud slides and lawsuits that go on for years. But he halted his weather report to come to grips with the flea and louse that had jumped from Silver onto the taller brother. He began to scratch first his wiry whiskers and then his throat with its necklace of grime.

To Silver's way of thinking, Armstrong was blessed with better luck than he, and also stronger arms. It was an incredible feat to cling to a chassis for at least fifteen minutes. Silver weighed the balance between luck and no luck. Maybe it was genetic. Not unlike his mother, Silver had bunions on his toes, a crooked spine, weeklong bouts with constipation, and feet that splayed out when he walked. At home, they shared the same ointments, vitamins, and chocolate-flavored laxatives. Maybe he had genetically picked up the propensity for bad love from his mother. In her own sorry love life, she had married an older man. Was he from Mexico? The Southwest? Timbuktu? He was anything but a doctor, an accountant,

or a chemist tossing back his powdery concoctions when
no one was in the room. He had the look of . . . Silver's
body jerked as he realized a truth at the end of a long day.
The person they buried was not his grandfather but his
father. He was the man in the wedding portrait, a fake as
far as Silver was concerned. All those years his mother
had referred to him as his grandfather. Not true. He was
his father.

"Jesus Christ," Silver scolded.

"Say it, my friend!" the brother hollered. He had un-
buttoned his shirt collar to round up the flea on his chest.

"Jesus!"

"Praise the King!"

Silver's hands went into his hair.

"That's a good sign! Pull at the roots! Jesus listens
when you got your own hair in your hand. He know suffering!" He scratched his scalp viciously. "I myself got
bugs on me!"

Silver abstained from talking about head lice with his
cell mate. He moaned from the edge of his cot, his face
buried in his palms. He reconstructed the face he had seen
in the wedding portrait. He saw the young face of his
mother and the then middle-aged face of his grandfather,
a person he saw only a few times. But it *was* his father.
Why didn't his mother tell him? When Silver got out of
his current hole, he was going to find out. He stood up,

his butt sore; he had known sandwiches that were thicker than his mattress. That cot embodied the best of the Spanish Inquisition.

"Let me out!" Silver screamed.

"Nah, man, go back to Jesus," scolded his cell mate. "That's the only way out. You can be in jail, outta jail, and Jesus will do time with you."

Silver ignored the advice. He preferred superheroes. If only he could bend the bars and smash the iron door with his fist. If only he could dissolve into a vapor and float out of the city jail, then reassemble into human form in front of a *taquería*. He was resolved to find out about his past but also to do something about his hunger.

Silver recalled some of the *pinto* poets he had met over the years. Secretly he believed they were lousy writers and full of exaggeration—sex was taking place around the clock from what they described. But it seemed to be true. Silver trembled at a moan in the cell at the farthest corner, and he prayed that the poor fellow was suffering from a toothache, not exploratory research conducted on him by a larger fellow. He flinched when he heard at the end of something painful, "Next."

The jail doors opened and closed all night, bringing in more sad souls with drink on their breath and pee steaming from their crotches. Luckily Silver shared his cell with a lone drunk. He was grateful for this as he lay in his bunk, scratching. At dawn, after the fleas and lice had drained his neck and spotted his throat with hickies, Silver showed a red eye to the new day. It was the worst sleep of his life. He opened both eyes and cleaned his face with the washrag of his two palms. He yawned and nearly choked on his yawn when he realized that that morning he was supposed to meet Linda at Starbucks. At nine, he recalled.

"Good God!" he hollered.

His cell mate for the night stirred. His feet stuck up into the air, his toenails like spurs on a rooster. His mouth was an open wound that would not heal no matter how he swabbed it with the alcohol of peach brandy.

Silver kicked off his blanket and shuffled to the toilet in the corner that had gargled a horrible human waste all night. The toilet was like an animal, breathing in and out, sighing through the rusty pipes. When Silver unzipped, careful not to touch his member with his dirty fingers, he didn't dare observe where he splashed. He didn't bother to flush, either, convinced that the toilet would throw up its dark contents.

Silver called, "Let me out!"

His cry echoed, but no one came.

Rattling the bars, Silver yelled, "I got a breakfast date."

His cell mate sat and rubbed his face with the washrags of *his* own palms. His eyes were jaundiced from drink and a bacterial affliction from street living. He got up and stag-

gered in his bare feet to the toilet, where he unzipped
and poured out peach brandy and whatever other liquids he brought into his body the night before. Then
he extended a foot. With his feet around the chrome
handle, he flushed for a good ten seconds. The animal
inside the toilet moaned loudly and seemed to cry a
name that sounded like "Naasswaaa." Slowly a dark
mush began to rise and spill over the bowl. A stench
rose like the dead into their cell. Silver placed a hand
over his mouth and nose. What rancid pigs' feet,
crawdads, boiled eggs, anchovies, and *chicharrones* did
a person have to eat to produce that smell?

"Police," Silver yelled when his cell mate, slow to
step, saw his feet sprinkled with the mush that had hit
the floor. The toilet came alive, boisterous. Soon there
followed pickle-shaped turds and other human waste,
then, mysteriously, a set of dentures that floated to the
top and sat precariously on the lidless rim before its grin
fell onto the floor.

"Don't call the pigs," the cell mate screamed, now
quickly shuffling backward in a Michael Jackson moon
walk. "Call Roto Rooter! Shit like black lava!" The cell
mate pointed at the dentures. "What the fuck's that,
man? Look like teeth. What they do, stuff a man down
that toilet?"

"Police!" Silver yelled again. He was scared that

eyeballs might start rolling out of the dark matter or a skeleton, stripped of flesh, might appear searching for its dentures.

"I ain't going to drink no more," the cell mate promised. Storklike, he wiped the muck from the toes of his left foot on the back of his pants leg.

"I hear you," Silver said. He promised himself that if he got out of this mess, he would write better poems.

Silver and the brother backed away from the spillage slowly mapping out the entire floor, sending the dentures riding a dark wave in their direction. Silver was envious that his cell mate had those incredible toenails to wrap around the lowest bars of the cell, where the two hung, yelling for the first time in their lives for the police. In this position, the men got to talk shit and know each other.

At ten-thirty, Silver learned that the grandson or son, the mysterious Mr. Gomez or whoever he was, was not going to press charges of trespassing. This news came by way of the jailer who had moved him and his cell mate, Lawrence Sewell, he learned during their ordeal, to the drunk tank, where every jailbird was preoccupied with fleas and lice, some of whom had ripped open their shirts and were like cats throwing their faces into their armpits and nibbling away at the itch. One brother, however, was overwhelmed by the phantoms that flashed in his eyes; he hadn't had a swig in twelve hours.

Silver was released after he signed forms in triplicate—the city wouldn't have to serve him lunch. One Salisbury steak was saved for a brother picked up for loitering with pissed pants on a commercial street corner during rush hour.

Silver stood outside the police department, pulling up the collar of his jacket that had seen both burial and jail time. The flagpole was banging its chain. Clouds, dark as anvils, were pushing eastward. He hustled to Starbucks and found Linda wasn't seated on a high stool, dutifully waiting. At *their* table sat two young women, their eyebrows tortured with safety pins. He circled the establishment and waited outside the women's rest room for ten minutes. When she didn't come out, he wondered if he could sue the city for the alienation of affection.

From Starbucks, Silver sprinted to Hardwick College, where he hollered to be let in. He had lost his key and nearly his mind. Now he needed a hypnotist to rid him of the nightmare he had witnessed in the great volume of shit spilling from the toilet.

"Felipe," he yelled over and over until a policeman across the street had grown tired of his pleas and warned him to shut up or else.

Posthaste, Silver got out of there. He paced Broadway Avenue, where every third person resembled Armstrong. The night before, Silver had bitterly called him a coward, among other outbursts, and then rightly corrected his view by admitting that he was just plain wise for not crawling out from underneath the Volvo and helping him with the police. He already had missing teeth. Why would he want to drop others?

Silver plunged his hands into both pants pockets of his suit. He brought forth a slip of paper that read Inspected by No. 14. He also brought forth lint pilfered from the depths of the corners. Neither helped his circumstance. God, if he only had Linda's telephone number.

En route home, he stopped for five minutes to admire a huge machine siphoning water from a clogged drain. But he moved on when the machine began to make an awful gurgling noise reminiscent of the frightening toilet in jail. With the sun momentarily out, it appeared he was following his own thin shadow, a compass of sort. It gave him direction.

Outside the bustle of downtown Oakland his ears filled with the music of shopping carts rattling glass and crushed beer and soda cans. He walked past the recycling center, where most everyone wore a wool beanie. And those without beanies had hair so nappy or long that no cold air could dislodge the warmth from their skulls.

His mother wasn't home. The windows were dark, although when Silver pressed his ear to the front door he made out the ticktock of the clock on the television. The refrigerator clicked on and the telephone rang three times, then stopped. He suspected that his mother was hiding somewhere in the shadows, or perhaps knitting quietly by the dim light of her own eyes. But most likely she was still at work, her eyeglasses fogged up from the large vats of boiling water. Soon her Dodge Colt would come rolling into the driveway. He would wait.

In the backyard, he tried the door to the garage; it was locked. He swept water from a lawn chair and sat down, his hands in his pockets against a wind blowing from the east. He was hungry. He hadn't eaten since morning, and that had been a single fried egg and a piece of toast.

"Come on, Mom," he said absently.

All he required was Linda's telephone number, written he believed on a piece of binder paper in his bedroom. The telephone number was also at Felipe's, but where was he? At the bank, licking his thumb as he counted out his loot from the stock market? Then he remembered Felipe's Volvo at his father's house. Woefully, he accommodated in his heart a tenderness toward Felipe, who was probably ghosting up and down a disheveled street, crying, "Silver, where's my car?"

He reprimanded himself; he was a fool. This was not an absentminded pronouncement, but at that late hour true as the rain that had begun to fall thunderously on the aluminum patio roof. He moved the lawn chair under the roof. The rain flogged the already soggy ground before it slowed to a steady beat. Silver was aware that the earth could swallow any and all bodies, but how much rain could it drink? To him, it had been raining more than forty days.

The neighbor's cat leapt from the fence to the ground to hear the proclamation of "I'm a fool" trumpeted from Silver's throat a second and third time. The cat nudged against Silver's leg, and its warmth changed the climate of his loneliness. The warmth reminded him of Spain and prodded Silver to reach in his shirt pocket for the letter from Profesora Olga Alvarez Moreno: This letter, like his key, was back at Hardwick College, tucked in a rumpled shirt that needed a good dunking in one of his mother's industrial laundry vats.

To add to the cat's warmth, Silver conjured up Spain: It was April in Madrid. He was seated at a large oak table surrounded by Chicano and Spanish poets, debating a smallish point, like the use of sparrows in poetry. He saw arguments flare and die like a campfire, and hours later, after their talk became civil, men and women offered *abrazos* of companionship and agreed that sparrows were small yet noble creatures worthy of poetry. He saw himself depart with Linda to bask in the afternoon sunlight and toast their fortunes by tipping back a bottle of wine.

Silver caught himself sighing. "Jesus, Lord, let me go to Spain. Let me have Linda." In saying this, he attained the status of a simple man yearning for nothing more than love. He would have fallen to his knees, except the ground was cold cement.

The cat meowed its own regrets.

His mother's car pulled into the garage, its yellowish headlight drooping and seemingly tired from the work-day. The car door opened and closed with a soft click. Although Silver was shivering, he wasn't in a hurry to knock on the door and confront his mother about *her* past. Who was that man we put in the grave yesterday? Would he rise on the third day and haunt Silver for the rest of his life? He petted the cat, who was suited up in thick black-and-white fur. The cat was warmer than he, better fed because no matter where he playfully poked the furry beast in its arms, legs, and belly, Silver detected layers of fat. In spite of the flecks of mud on his paws, the cat was well groomed and with a tiny bell on his reflec-tor collar—he had a home to return to on cold nights. Silver had none.

The kitchen light came on, illuminating the side of

the yard with a cool radiance. When the refrigerator opened with a pucker, the cat turned its head sharply toward the back door. Silver made out the bang of a kettle: His mother was boiling water for tea.

Silver pushed himself out of the lawn chair, shaking the spittle of rainwater from his pants cuffs, and headed to the back door. He knocked. His mother's face appeared immediately behind a curtain. She seemed startled, as if she had just woken suddenly from sleep and was assessing her whereabouts.

"What are you doing here?" she asked after she struggled with the warped door. Her voice was flat, though not mean. Behind her shoulder steam was rising from the kettle. She held the door open for Silver.

"We need to talk, Mom."

He entered the house, slipping out of his shoes for fear of tracking dirt into the house. His face was lost in the steam as he passed through the kitchen into the living room, where he undid the strap to his trench coat and slipped out of it. His mother didn't follow her son right away. Silver heard her go through a cupboard, moving the spices like chess pieces, and bring down the sugar bowl. He heard the dunking splash of a tea bag in two cups, the chiming ring of a spoon against the mugs, silence, and finally the shuffle of her feet as she advanced slowly into the living room. She was carrying two Mickey

Mouse mugs.

"I'll get it," he said, rising to meet his mother. He took a cup and carefully set it on the hill of his knee. He sneezed from the quick climate change of cold to warm.

His mother turned on the lamp, but its light hardly lit the walls. The light fell to the floor and was absorbed into the dark carpet. Still, she noticed his smashed nose. "Does it hurt?" Her eyes were more weary than dilated with concern.

Silver was uncertain if she meant his nose or the larger issue of life itself. He shook his head. He allowed her to sip and complain that the tea lacked sugar. Her mouth was a wound of lines when she bunched her lips and blew on the undrinkable hot tea. He struck with a direct question: "Was that my father we buried?"

His mother's mouth fell open, shaking out the lines of old age. She averted her eyes. She placed her mug down, and her left hand reached for the right. It was as if they needed to be held and since she had no one, her own hands leapt to each other for comfort. The right hand pecked at the left, like a bird.

"You knew I would find out," Silver claimed. "Is that why you sent me to his house? To find out on my own?" He moved his mug from his knee to the coffee table. "You couldn't tell me to my face?"

"I just couldn't." When she lowered her gaze, the shadows rolled on her lined face, eclipsing what light had brightened her skin. "It was too hard for me."

"And life ain't hard for me?" He threw up his hands, and his lap caught them on the way down.

When she lifted her face, the shadows stayed under her eyes. "He wasn't your grandfather, like you say. He was my cousin."

Silver's puzzled face searched for an explanation.

His mother said it all. "I fell in love with my cousin. He was older than me." She hesitated. "Well, it wasn't love. Maybe it was desperation to get out of the house."

Silver's face remained puzzled.

His mother picked up her mug, put it back down. Her shoulders jerked as she piped up a cry that might have been lodged inside her for years. "I didn't know he had a wife in Mexico. I didn't know a lot of things, *mi'jo*. I was seventeen."

"How old was he?"

She wiped her eyes, as if trying to rid herself of the present scene. "I don't know. Thirty-six?"

Silver's eyebrows rose and fell. He wrung his hands. "I can't believe it. I used to visit him and he never said anything about being my father."

His mother shrugged. It was the left hand's turn to peck at the right.

"Not once!"

She shrugged a second time.

The two sat in silence. The cat that Silver had petted for warmth was at the front door. It meowed and then stopped.

"Mom, I'm sorry for you." He got up, edged a place next to her on the couch, and hugged her for the first time in many years. Her bones were the bones of a stranger. He hugged her until her crying slowed to a whimper and the cat's meowing could be made out once more. Silver got up and fetched a paper towel for her eyes and nose. He was dazed. My father was also my second cousin?

"Who was the man I saw?" Silver asked when he returned from the kitchen. "He turned me in to the cops."

She looked up. Her face was shiny as the sea. "What man? The police arrested you?"

Silver didn't wish to disturb her any more. He was troubled by the person named Gomez, the man who had seized the box of photographs. He asked, "The guy's name is Gomez."

His mother smothered her face in the paper towel. "He's your brother."

"Oh, Jesus," a bewildered Silver moaned. Why had he asked?

"Not your real brother," she continued. "Your half brother. Your father, like I said, he had a wife in Mexico.

That's one of the sons."

"Are there more of them?" He pictured six Gomezes, all pleated with age and sporting wiry mustaches.

She nodded with the paper towel still pressed to her face. Through that veil, she told him that some of the sons had died, but she believed that most of them were alive. Alfredo Gomez, the one Silver had met, had settled in California in the 1960s. He was a janitor at a school in San Jose; this much she knew. "He's just like his father— stingy." She sniffled after she made this confession: "Even worse than me."

Silver rose and sat back in the chair across from her. "So this guy wants the house?"

She nodded. The paper towel had come down from her face and was crushed in her fist. She was seated in front of Silver, telling him the truth. And the truth, he found out, hurt.

"I could smack him!" Silver snarled. He was thirty-nine and had never hit another adult, other than the accidental eye poke to Al. He could begin with this man.

His mother whimpered, as if she had been smacked.

"Let him have the house and photos and whatever shit he wants!" Silver pictured the house crumbling in the next earthquake. Usually nonviolent, he pictured the refrigerator falling on this person's cow-shaped head.

"Mom, is your maiden name Mendez?"

She nodded.

This part was solved. But Silver was curious if his birth certificate included the last name of Gomez. But he would bring this up later, perhaps when his mother returned to form and was once again spitting pins at him in anger about one thing or another.

"I'm sorry to tell you," his mother finally said, which was something of an apology. A fresh burst of tears accumulated on her cheeks, adding to her apology.

Silver picked up his mug of tea. He raised it high, as if toasting this piece of news. He took a sip of the cooled-down liquid: mint-flavored tea.

His mother got up, sighing, and went into the kitchen. He heard her pull another paper towel from the dispenser over the toaster. Silver imagined her drying her tears and then using the same towel to wipe down the counter.

While she was cooking their dinner, Silver retrieved Linda's telephone number in his room and called her. He got her on the third ring. "Linda, it's me."

Linda was silent on the other end. Silver saw her chewing a loop of her hair with her teeth.

"I'm sorry about this morning."

"I waited for you." Her voice tried to rise in scorn, but her mood was anything but. She sounded concerned.

Silver promised to explain later. When Linda said that she wanted to hear right now and then, Silver swallowed and whispered, "I just buried my mom's cousin." He felt a knob of sorrow grow in his throat as he swallowed a second time. "And my father, too."

Silver also promised himself to watch Mexican *telenovelas* to learn about his culture. He recalled snickering at a few episodes of one program or another, laughing meanly because the family structures in these half-hour programs were preposterous and melodramatic. Now he wasn't so sure.

Before dinner, he stripped off the suit and bathed in water hot enough to scald the feathers off a fat hen. When he exited the bathroom, steam curling behind him, he discovered his mother had prepared him chicken mole, frijoles, and rice, riches for his stomach, which required a sumptuous meal after a long day of heartburn. Later he consoled and forgave his mother, as all the while the muted television brightened their faces with a burst of commercials. When she pressed a twenty-dollar bill into his hand, he could only offer further praise for her cooking. He advised her that she should forget her husband—his father, his cousin, his whatever—and her stepson, who, he rightly found, was greedy for an old house and a box of old photographs. Let him lift and carry away what he wanted.

"Mom, it's water under the bridge," Silver preached from the couch. He wasn't ashamed of this old metaphor that Moses might have used if he had not climbed the mountain but instead went down to the river. His poetic sensibility wasn't bothered either when he told her that every day she should wake up and smell the roses. He had to soothe her guilt. Today is the first day of the rest of your life, he argued with his hand in her hands. He sermonized that what goes up must come down. He scratched his head at this last saying. But he was confident in saying that the Gomez guy had made his own bed and he must lie in it with a smoldering cigarette. That night, he was a felon of a phrase maker.

He slept at his mother's house, and the next morning he woke early and got a ride with her to Hardwick College, his mother cooing that no, it wasn't out of her way. He was certain that it was—in the rearview mirror he spied the factories of Hayward, but they were headed to downtown Oakland, where the street commerce took the shape of shopping carts rolled by indigents. He hugged his mother awkwardly and assured her that he was on his way and that—a joke she didn't get, perhaps didn't appreciate—he was off to meet his smart friends.

"I'm sorry," his mother lamented. "I wish I had been a better mom."

"Nah, Mom, you were great." He saw pins shooting

from her mouth. What was a lie between a son and mother?

She pressed a paper bag into his chest. After he waved good-bye from the corner, his hand plunged into this bag: His fingers touched the cups of Linda's bra. He fought the urge to throw his face into the cups and breathe deeply. Instead he tightened the hold on the bag and walked briskly to Hardwick College.

When Silver began to tell his friend about his night in jail, Felipe put his hands over his ears. He was reluctant to know anything about anything. But he was glad to get his Volvo back, though he complained that Armstrong had brought it back empty of gas and with the steering wheel greasy.

But Felipe was curious. "Yeah, your friend said that you might be in trouble with the police."

Silver envisioned Lieutenant Waldman with three doughnuts around his huge thumb. "Nah, not really."

Felipe pointed at the bag. "What do you have there?"

"A bra."

"Ah, Silver, you're not cross-dressing, are you?"

"Nah, homes, I'm superstraight." But Silver did have to admit he did like the smoothness of panties.

Felipe next brought up another piece of news: "Your friend took all the clothes."

"The clothes?"

"In the old store. Down below."

Silver pictured an empty stockroom. He pictured every black and brown brother wearing out-of-date clothes and ghosting around downtown Oakland. This disturbed Silver momentarily because the letter from Profesora Alvarez Moreno was riding in the breast pocket of his shirt, the one with elephant ear lapels. But he still had her e-mail address and a buddy with a computer.

When Silver clip-clopped downstairs in Felipe's large slippers and pushed open the storage room, he discovered the entire inventory of clothes was gone. Only dust floated across the room and sunlight sparkled like a belt buckle from a hole in the curtain. In a way, Silver felt robbed, a victim. Then he disputed his thoughts: Maybe Armstrong was a saint plotting his entrance into heaven by distributing his meager findings to the poor. He returned upstairs, where he brushed his teeth and splashed his throat with cologne. He lay on his sleeping bag, his fingers laced, and prayed that he could swoop up Linda into his arms. He realized that *swoop* was the wrong word; she was a heavy angel. He settled for the word *lead*.

Silver rested and then consulted the two clocks in the room: eight twenty-three, thirty-seven minutes before their new rendezvous at Starbucks. He rose and smoothed the sleeping bag, where he intended to lower Linda romantically if his lower back didn't cause him much pain. It still hurt from the scuffle with the police.

Silver returned to Felipe's office. "I'm going out. You know where my key is?"

Felipe shrugged but offered him another one on a rabbit's foot.

"Linda," he caught himself whispering as he ran his thumb against the grain of the rabbit's foot, then with the grain. Either way, it gave his thumb pleasure to touch something furry.

Silver descended and stood on the steps of the college. A huge dark cloud plugged the hole where the sun had shone earlier. He went forth, watching a plume of his breath dance in the cold air. He was happy. He gave no regard to a man chipping a brick from the side of the building. He scooped at his white breath and philosophized as he left Hardwick College that poetry was nothing but words made of breathy exhaust.

At the city-made lake, he praised the geese that craned their faucetlike necks when he called, "Let's eat, little brothers." This morning he came prepared for his feathered friends. He brought from his pocket bread that he broke apart and sprinkled for the geese, who seemed to be smirking. That's how their bills were shaped—*smirk, smirk, smirk* as they gobbled what he had placed religiously on the water.

Silver was distracted by the bark of a street merchant across the street. The man had fixed an emporium of clothes on a chain-link fence—shirts, pants, vests and sweaters, and entire suits all like flags rippling in wind. He had dozens of shoes moored against the fence. A set of ties resembled the tails of floundering kites.

It was Armstrong, a street merchant.

For six seconds, Silver struggled with the urge to greet his friend, to tell him, "I got out of jail, safe and sound." He remained cautious because he was not going to risk missing his nine o'clock date with Linda. But he took a defensive step in Armstrong's direction when a police cruiser rolled up. An officer got out, kicking back his hat with a nudge of his hand, baffled.

"Damn," Silver cussed. He crossed the street and edged close enough to hear Armstrong yell to the cop, "I ain't doing nothing but selling funeral suits." He smiled and adjusted a colorful tie on his thin neck.

"Good God," Silver whispered.

Armstrong spread open his trench coat. "See, I'm wearing one myself. People need to go in style."

Silver was confused. Did Armstrong mean the people who were being buried or those mourners who huddled like pigeons around a dropped thing? Either way, the reference was death.

The cop said something Silver couldn't make out. But he heard Armstrong say, "Me and Mr. Moses Thatchgill got a business operation and he a member of the black,

Hispanic, and white chamber of commerce."

The cop warned Silver, not Armstrong, that he had better be gone by end of the day and got back into his cruiser. He was serving the community by leaving it alone.

It was a relief to Silver that he didn't have to get involved. He had his date with Linda, and time, like a pencil sharpener, was cranking out dead minutes. He bid farewell to the geese and walked in the direction of Starbucks, his steps quickening as they obeyed his racing heart.

"It's her," Silver said, his eyes beaded against the glare of rainwater shining up from the gutter. He found himself running but slowed to a brisk walk when he saw that she was moving quickly toward him, a curious experience because most of his friends and acquaintances usually sped the other way. He recalled a high school math problem: If a train is traveling at fifty miles per hour from Bakersfield and another train is traveling in its direction from Sacramento at sixty, how long will it take them to meet? He was unable to calculate the answer but regarded a safety measure: Close your eyes when trains collide. He resembled a locomotive, his breath issuing skyward. Linda's breath was chugging skyward as well, a sign that she was out of shape.

"Linda," he called as he once again started running.

Linda, arms outstretched, brought Silver into her body. She planted a kiss on his neck and then one on his mouth.

She caught her breath and asked: "Do you like this, Mr. Poetry Lover?"

Was there ever an easier answer? "Yes, a lot."

Linda touched his face. "What happened to your nose?

"It got smashed."

She raised a worried eyebrow. "Poor baby, tell me about it?"

"It was a cops-and-robbers thing." He said it was nothing and that in a week he would again be able to pick up the aroma of perfume and home cooking. He was happy, a small-press poet on a street where city workers were in a hurry, it being the first of the month, and paychecks in brown envelopes were waiting.

"Come on," she commanded after she fixed another red kiss on his neck.

They entered Starbucks, moist with the smell of coffee and wet wool coats, and claimed the table where a few days ago they sat, pleading their cases whether they were lovers or former lovers. Silver blew on the pastry crumbs on the table. Linda worked a curl behind her ear. Playfully Silver inquired if she was beckoning for him to kiss her there.

"No," she answered. "It's a sign for me to hear about . . ."

"My father," he concluded for her. His attention was drawn over to the counter, where the bleary-eyed coffee drinkers were lined up, some of them full of jitters for their morning fix. He ignored her questions. He asked: "Do you want a latte?" The twenty-dollar bill from his mother was in his pocket and ready to break itself into small denominations. He was ready to splurge.

"No, I'm fine right now." But she slid off her stool and got them two small paper cups of water from a plastic pitcher. They drank them empty.

Linda again asked about his father.

Clouds rolled over the light in Silver's eyes. He munched on his lips, a habit of his in her presence. He threw his hands up into the air and his lap caught them. This, too, had become a habit, his hands flying like hurt birds. "Sweetie, not now. I can't explain."

Linda darkened with hurt.

"Really, Linda, I can't right now." He labored against arguing that it was similar to her talking about Al two days after his death. Also, he was scared that he might scare her away if he told her that his mother bedded down with her cousin and the result was him, a poet without a rock to call a pillow.

Linda's mood brightened as she squeezed Silver's arm. She was like flowers in his face. "Silver, you tell me when you want." She ran her hands through his hair. "Tell Mommy what you want."

Silver smiled boyishly. "I would, but it's really silly."

He would have installed a blush on his face but didn't have time because Linda cooed, "You tell your poor mommy girl anything you want."

"You're my mommy girl?" Silver asked. Yesterday he would have felt stupid talking baby gibberish. Now he was loving it.

Linda waited for his answer.

He licked his lips, giving his tongue something to do other than swamp her ears with kisses. He wished that he had stuck with guitar to sing his love. His rickety voice would do. "I want you to be my poetry."

She laughed until her earrings chimed. "That's a pretty silly line." She embraced Silver. "But it will do for now." She threw her face like a hatchet into his neck and worked from left to right planting kisses.

Neither ordered coffee. They gave up their table to a herd of happy city workers with paychecks in their wallets. They were boisterously debating the sweet tastes of muffins, pound cakes, and éclairs.

Instead of steering themselves directly to Hardwick College, his sanctuary, not counting the occasional rendezvous with loneliness at the bus station, he steered Linda into a Chinese bakery and bought pork buns and ginseng sodas. He planned to use most, if not all, of his morning calories from his mother's breakfast of eggs by making love to Linda. His secret design was to replenish his drive with this little snack and do it again. His further design was to tell her about his family—mother, father, this guy named Gomez—in the days to come. But that family heritage could wait.

"Is this a loft?" she asked of Hardwick College when he called into the intercom and then remembered the key Felipe had given him. Linda took three steps backward and looked up, a hand over her brow in a salute. "How come bricks are missing?"

"It's a long story," Silver answered hurriedly. He wanted to see her naked as quickly as possible. "It's just an old building. It's got a language school on the third floor, and me and Felipe share a place on the fifth." The two climbed the stairs to the third floor, and when Silver sang, "Knock knock" at the open door, Felipe stood up like a gentleman, wiped crumbs of powdery white doughnut from the front of his shirt, and shook Linda's hand lightly.

"This is the man," Silver said.

Felipe beamed.

Silver pointed at the computer screen with its colored graphs of stocks. "This is what Felipe does."

"Well, yes, but I also teach English." He was embarrassed about his on-line day trading.

The three stood in silence.

"I'm going to be busy for a while," Silver said after a

moment, believing that he was being subtle, if not noble. But he fooled no one, including Linda, who pulled on Silver's arm and cried, "Let's go!"

They climbed the stairway to the fifth floor with Linda eagerly leading the way. Wind and sunlight entered the window at the end of the hall. Silver was thankful for that sign of sunlight. Perhaps a rainbow was brightening the streets in the not too far distance.

"This is our place." He pushed open the door. "No one lives up here. And downstairs is like a morgue, too." He could have bitten his tongue for the reference to the morgue.

"Not bad, for two guys," Linda remarked. She ignored his slip of the tongue.

The room was tidy with a single bed, a table, the two clocks, and books both on the shelf and in boxes. Silver turned on one of their two floor lamps, its yellowish light warm against the gray walls. Silver shed his coat and helped Linda with hers. They were not bashful lambs, nor tigers with their claws out and scratching for meat. They faced each other and embraced. Their arms roamed up and down and, slowly, like camels, they lowered themselves to their knees on the unzipped sleeping bag.

"Love can be easy," Linda panted.

Easy was a word he was beginning to fit into his vocabulary. Even her buttons were slipping out of their holes with his lightest touch.

They kissed and groped each other. Silver worked on one button after another on her blouse. He repeated her name over and over and thanked God for the inch of cotton that clogged his lumpy sleeping bag. Such padding was all they needed.

"Do you like this?" Linda panted.

Only a fool would answer.

"I thought of you a lot of times, Silver." She had undone her bra, and the heaviness of her breasts rolled on her belly. He stuttered when she opened her legs. The kingdom of hair was astonishing. When he lowered himself to his knees, she opened her legs even more, a gesture of "come on, lover boy." The experience was new and the feeling was so powerful that he had to close his eyes to deepen this rocking that he hadn't known in years.

Afterward they slept, woke, and made love a second time. Linda cried. She said she felt awful, a word that she repeated until her face changed and became stern. She told Silver about three children Al had fathered, including one who was at the funeral.

"His son was at the funeral?" Silver rose to his elbow. He was curious.

"Yeah." But she didn't offer any details. Instead she played with the beads of her necklace like a rosary.

"I'm happy," Silver said, touching the beads.

"No, you're silly, Yum-yum Boy," she countered playfully. That was to be his new name. She wiped a tear from her cheek and hugged Silver. She darted her tongue behind his ear and whispered, "You're so skinny, Yum-yum Boy."

Silver bathed in the glory of his new title. He liked how she rose bashfully and stepped into her panties, white as Kleenex. She struggled with the bra, and he almost said, "I have one just like that," but he just rolled onto his back. His smoky stare lighted on the paper bag where her bra was. He told himself, When she's gone, I'm going to massage those empty cups. Hell, I might even wear them!

"Get dressed, Yum-yum Boy," she told Silver.

Silver laced his hands behind his head. "Why?"

She slipped into her slacks and blouse and put on the earrings she had taken off. "Because you've been lost for a long time, and it's time to go home."

For the next few weeks, at a one-bedroom basement apartment on Telegraph Avenue in Berkeley, Silver fattened up on lovemaking and an array of goodies in the refrigerator. The bananas and apples in a bowl didn't have much of a chance of survival. The cheeses were cut into square planks, set on Wheat Thins, and gobbled up. They ate pasta salad, rice of varied grains, and noodles fat as pencils. Silver loved his marvelous new life in a clean bed. He cuddled a cat named Smudge, a name he enjoyed because it was anything but a smudge: Checkered white and black, he matched the floor of Linda's kitchen.

"We're on an ark," Silver told Linda, who, in this cold off-season, tampered with a new line of jewelry; she replaced the edible jewelry with pieces made of iron and bronze. She worked with a small chrome hammer and a soldering iron. A tray of beads brightened the table. Silver felt kingly when Linda brought home sacks of used clothes from the Salvation Army—three pairs of pants, an unused belt, shirts starched and crisp as freshly minted dollar bills, and a checkered black-and-white sweater. When Silver wore it and carried Smudge around the apartment, they blended together like camouflage. Linda changed his name from "Yum-yum Boy" to "Skinny Kitty," a description that became less apt as his waist began to thicken, a tom-tom she played before and after their lovemaking.

Silver managed to do two poetry readings at community colleges, each paying five hundred dollars, readings that would not happen until late March. But it was money in the bank, so to speak. He applied for and received a new passport. Revived, Silver began a series of love poems titled "The Ark." The wind howled and bent the trees and threw down traffic lights. The Oakland airport closed down for two days; city workers in yellow slickers vacuumed water and leaves from manholes and clogged gutters.

Silver revealed for Linda the embroiled history of his grandfather, a title that was anything but true. His father was his mother's cousin, who was an old man when they became lovers. He told her about the photographs he discovered at his father's house and his father's son, Gomezwhatever, and his arrest and detention, where the fleas and lice brought out their swords and lances to poke at his neck. Linda listened with her mouth open, as she was readying to resuscitate Silver if he began to choke on his story. That evening, Linda made him meat loaf, a comfort food.

In late March, after the rains had receded and his college readings had come and gone, Silver applied with gusto a fistful of rags to the Camaro. He polished the car not once but twice and blackened the tires with hair dye found under the sink in the bathroom. He attended first to the engine—changed the oil, changed the air and gas filters. He flushed the radiator, added antifreeze, and scraped corrosion from the battery cables. He replaced two tires with recaps and scrubbed the grime from the steering wheel, grime built up from Al's palms beating out rhythms. He polished the car and made a sign to place inside the windshield—$1200.

He drove the Camaro to a corner off Telegraph and Fifty-fifth Street—a high-visibility location—and was locking up the vehicle when Rolando and Victor Chabran rolled out of the Wee Little Bar, once an Irish pub but now the haunt of riffraff of every color.

"Hey, it's the poet," Rolando shouted. He was hanging on to Victor, who had thicker legs and thus was responsible for leading them in a balancing act to their parked truck. His eyes were spiked red, as if he had poured Bloody Marys straight into their sockets.

"Shit," Silver swore under his breath. His first option was to slide into the car and drive away, but his second was to hold his ground. It was wait and see.

Rolando steadied his watery gaze on the Camaro. "Hey, ain't that Al's ride?"

Victor pushed his brother away. "Stupid, Al can't ride no more. Not where he is."

"Where is he?" Rolando asked.

"Man, I gotta hit you," Victor growled. With his palm slap to the chest, he thumped his brother, who staggered backward three steps and fell to the ground. Rolando grimaced and hammered the sidewalk with his fist. "That's right, Al's dead."

"*No respeto,*" Victor hollered. "You're a drunk Mexican."

"I got *mi respeto*," Rolando barked. He cupped a hand around his crotch, damp from a night and day drinking not a Wee Little but a Whole Lot.

Victor jumped on his brother and the two rolled like bears. Seeing it as his cue, Silver slyly got into the car, started up the engine, and drove away, his eyes on the rearview mirror. He watched the image of the Chabran brothers get smaller and smaller until they disappeared for good.

The Camaro sold for $950, and that money, along with a thousand from Linda, plus what remained of the poetry-reading checks, was presented to Felipe, who worked his magic. By the end of three days, he had earned them six thousand dollars and enjoyed the right to shake a finger at Silver and warn him, no, scold him that he had better see that the tax was paid on his earnings. The government was cracking down on day traders. Tax cheats were singing behind bars from morning to night.

For years, Silver revered death as an end, but with the departure of Al and Silver's father, he saw it as a beginning. He mulled this notion as the five-engine 757 rode a whip-ass wind at thirty-five thousand feet above the Atlantic. Linda gripped his hands at the slightest turbulence. He laid his face into her neck, a cove that solved all his problems. They were on their way to Spain, where—God, yes—they were going to sit in a patch of sunlight and sip from a bottle of red wine at their feet. Silver promised to learn more about wine and more about Linda, who sparkled with jewelry and a pinprick of light in her eyes. She still cried in her sleep for Al, but she also had an equal flow of tears of joy for Silver.

With his tray table down, Silver composed while flying through a cargo of clouds but stopped when he wrote, "The ark, that slick, slick boat, rides the waters of life." He clacked the pen between his upper and lower teeth, ambivalent to the line's meaning. He didn't worry. His poetry, after all, was Linda. He would complete a new book of poems on the other side of the world. He peered out the small portal by the window seat. Down below, the ocean offered up fish, the dolphin and the porpoise, a whale in the distance, and, as he saw through the glare of sun on water, row upon row of waves, white tipped and beautifully endless.